Something like Love

Gyan Singh

Invincible Publishers

First published in India in 2017 by Invincible Publishers

 2nd Edition 2017
ISBN: 978-93-86148-94-0

Digitally Printed at Replika Press Pvt. Ltd.

Invincible Publishers
G-120, Sushant Lok III, Sector 57, Gurgaon-122002

DEDICATION

To my small town Daltonganj and all my DAVians

Acknowledgment

* * *

Thank you dear readers and friends for picking up 'Something Like Love'.

First of all, I would like to thank Lord Shiva and Maa Parvati for their blessings.

I would particularly like to thank:

- Invincible publications for considering my manuscript Aditi Saxena, for helping me with the editing and Sneha Agrawal for designing the cover and layout.
- My parents and family for their support.
- Madan Verma of *Gyan Niketan* for his support.
- Mantu bhaiya who suggested that I write this novel in the first place.
- Nidhi and Kriti, because they always encouraged me to write.

- Suyash, Ankit, Chanchal, Utkarsh and all my dear DA-Vians.
- Chandan Dubey and Jeet Prakash for their support.
- Kaushal, Alok and Anjali from IIMT engineering college.

Special gratitude does out for:

- Sunil Vishwakarma sir of M.K. DAV for his encouragement.
- Archana ma'am and Alok Garg sir for their encouragement.
- Srishty, because her words changed the direction of this novel.
- Aashish Bhardwaj for his support and Sweta Pandey for her encouragement.
- A muslim girl.
- Suraj Sir, Ravi Sir, both chief officers, Krishna Mohan sir and Arun Sir. Cadets and all the crew members of the first ship BC CHATTERJEE for their support in writing this book.

Something Like Love

* * *

The road was almost deserted like the head of a widow. Only a few vehicles could be seen passing by. It was hardly eight, but the night of January compelled everyone to pack themselves in their houses early. There was a closed shop on the left side of the road. The board read "PRINCE GENERAL STORE, GANGA NAGAR, MEERUT," which was only visible in the dim light lit outside the shop.

Dense fog engulfed all around resisting visibility completely. In front of the shop, there was a giant gate, on top of which, 'IIMT ENGINEERING COLLEGE' was written. Three guards with guns on their shoulders, guarded at the gate.

"Why has Yogesh sir come to college now?" one of the guards said while sliding his hands deep into his pockets.

"Day after tomorrow is the cultural night. He might have come to check the arrangements," replied the other guard.

"He is the chairman of this college. He can come in whenever he wants to. Who are we to ask?" the third guard smiled while adjusting his gun.

Suddenly a car stopped and a man came out hurriedly.

He started running towards the gate. Guards who stood dull earlier became vigilant. The light of the two halogens which were fixed above the gate revealed his fair face clearly. He was tall and looked handsome in his clean shaven and well groomed self. The black suit which he wore reflected his striking personality. He had a book in his right hand.

"Excuse me sir. Where are you going?" One of the guards stopped him.

"What?" He startled. It seemed as if he had noticed the presence of the guards just then.

"Where are you going?" The three of them drew closer to him.

"Inside, " he replied fixated.

"Why?"

"She is waiting for me," he shouted, confused.

"At night, who?" one of the guards enquired.

"She...She is waiting. Please let me go," he moved ahead, pushing a guard. Two of thm ran and blocked his way. The third guard twisted his arm against his back.

"Sir you can't go this way, who do you want to meet?"

"Naghma... Naghma... is waiting for me, Please let me go," he tried to wrestle out of their grip.

"Sir, who is she? Does she live in the hostel? Tell me. I will call the warden," one of the guards tried to make him understand.

"Please let me go, she is waiting." He sat on the ground and started cringing.

"Sir, please wait, we can't allow you in. Please stand sir."

It was the effect of his car and personality that made

the guards call him 'sir' and even considering his plea, else they would have thrown him out.

Suddenly, he stood, pushed the two guards off and entered the gate. For a few seconds the guards didn't understand what had just happened, but when they came to their senses, they ran towards him and caught hold of him just a few metersafter the entrance.

"Naghma… Naghma…" He shouted as loud as he could. "Naghma… I am here Naghma…," he was struggling hard to get rid of their grip.

"What are you doing sir? Please stop," the guards were still trying to make him understand.

The chairman of IIMT ENGINEERING COLLEGE came out with three faculties. Since the cultural night was just a day after, some of the faculties were compelled to stay till late to accomplish all the arrangements. He heard the noise and his attention shifted towards the gate.

In his attempt to escape, he shrugged out of the coat that the guards gripped so tightly and stumbled forward. His head banged at the boundary wall of the parking. He fell down. All his protests ended suddenly. He lay there quietly. He didn't even try to stand up. By then Yogesh sir had also reached there.

"What happened?" He asked the guards.

"Sir, he was trying to get inside. We tried to stop but..." he was still holding that black suit in his hand.

"Why? Who is he?"He asked.

"We don't know sir. He was asking for some Naghma."

"Naghma…?" He whispered to himself and then said he must want to meet some girl from the hostel. There must be hundreds of Naghmas. Take him out and tell him to come tomorrow morning. Is he drunk?"

"Don't know sir, but his breath is not stinking." The

guards carried him out.

Yogesh sir turned to go, but suddenly his eyes caught the book which was lying where the guy had fallen. The name of the book was "First Love Will Always Be First, by Chandan Singh."

"Wait! Wait! Whose book is this?" Sir picked up the book. "This book was published three weeks ago and is getting a good response. I saw it in the news," Alok sir said looking at the faculties.

"Stop! Stop! Guards Stop!" he screamed suddenly. Everyone started looking at him surprised.

"Is he Chandan Singh, the writer of this book? See! See! His photo. He is the same guy. He gave the book to one of the faculty members."

"Take him to my cabin," sir told the guards.

"Oh! This is that Chandan," said Alok Garg, HOD of the Physics Department.

"Do you know him?" Yogesh sir asked him.

"He was in our college during first year," said Alok sir.

"He is asking about the Naghma from Muzaffar Nagar," said Saurav sir, faculty of EVS and Bioscience.

"Muzaffar Nagar, Naghma? Naghma of Muzaffar Nagar riot?" Yogesh sir startled.

"Yes sir," Archana ma'am, who was the cultural head, approved of the fact.

"How does he know her? What relation would he have with her? And why is he asking about her now?" It seemed Yogesh sir knew Naghma very well. He emphasized on the word now.

"They were studying in the same branch computer science and were always seen together, but unfortunately," Alok sir left the sentence hanging.

"Come let's see him. How is he?"Alok sir rushed

towards the campus. The other three faculties followed him.

They all were sitting around Chandan. He was laid unconscious on the bed.

"Call the doctor," ordered Yogesh sir.

A doctor was always there in the college campus for hostel students. He examined him and said, "Don't disturb him. He lost consciousness due to stress. He will regain his senses on his own, in time."

When the doctor left the room, Yogesh sir said, "What is in this novel? Is it about Nagma?"

"Can't say, Sir," Saurav sir shook his head.

"Let's read what is written in this?" Sir flapped the cover page of the book.

First Love will always be first

* * *

It was a pleasant evening and the sky was mildly cloudy. Wind was softly swaying the leaves of the trees. The reddish sun was ready to bid goodbye and hide itself in the west. There was huge traffic around me and I was struggling with the clutch and brake. My eyes cast on the indicator and my speedometer, which showed 30 km/hr. The brake light of the white 'Indigo', which was in front of me, glowed. My foot jammed down on the break pedal. The indicator dropped left to 20 km/hr. I was so annoyed with this traffic and wanted to be as far as possible from the madness. I wasn't out for work. I was driving only to enjoy the nature, and the romantic weather.

I managed somehow to drive out of the city and accelerated with receding traffic. I switched off the A.C. of my car and slid down the glass of the window on my right. Gusts of cold wind stroke my face.

The needle of the speedometer was dancing between 80-85 km/hr. The music system played a number sung by Lata Mangeskar. "LAG JA GALE KI FIR YE HASIN RAAT HO N' HO."

There was a turn ahead, but I didn't bother to slow down the speed of my car. I was never so careless, but perhaps the effect of the weather made me so careless that I turned my car without decreasing the speed while only blowing the horn.

"Carelessness is the first step of accident."

There was a scooty coming from the other side. I estimated the risk of collision, so I almost stood on the brake to avoid it. Tires screeched on the road, but the bumper of my car hit the scooty, and I saw a girl thrown up in the air due to the collision, before she fell on the side of the road. I opened the gate hurriedly and ran towards the girl. Her black scooty had fallen at the other side of the road. My heart was beating so loud, it rang in my ear. I was frightened.

I sat down, took her wrist in my hand and checked for pulse. I breathed a sigh of relief. But her condition deserved pity. Her head was bleeding badly because it had struck hard on the stony road. My right hand slid in my pocket and brought out a white handkerchief. I pressed it gently on the wound to resist bleeding, but in vain.

A quick thought flashed through my head, "Leave the girl and run away. If she dies, you would be confined by the police."

But another thought dismissed it. "She will die, everyone will leave her. No one wants to indulge themselves in a police case."

While these thoughts still wrestled in my head, I turned her over I felt like I had been stung by a scorpion. Her face made me gasp. I was petrified. I knew her, but never expected to meet her here, that too in this condition. Now there was no confusion in my mind. She had to be taken to the hospital and I had to do it. I did not have a bandage on me so I took off my shirt immediately and tied it over her wounded head tightly. I lifted her quickly in my arms and made her lie down on the back seat of my car.

I turned back towards the city. I was grateful that there was no traffic this time and I was in front of a hospital in the next twenty minutes.

I lifted her back in my arms. I was distraught, frightened and annoyed and ran towards the entrance of the hospital.

"It's an emergency, Sister, " I shouted on reaching the reception, where a woman was sitting in a white uniform.

"What happened to her? How did this happen?" she queried.

"Sister…" I was panting like a dog. "Sister, she fell from the stairs. She is my wife." I lied point blank. She was not my wife, but I did not want her to know about the accident because then she would call the police, which I never wanted.

She signalled at the two ward boys who were standing near the reception. They came with a stretcher and carried her from there. I also wanted to follow them, but the nurse stopped me.

"Sir, please fill this form," she requested. She was calm with no feelings and in no hurry. Perhaps because she faced such scenario every day. Such cases were common to her.

I filled in the forms immediately and handed them over to her.

"First floor emergency ward," she directed me to where I was most eager to go.

Instead of waiting for the lift I ran towards the stairs and reached at the emergency ward.. I wanted to enter, but one of the ward boys, who had taken her, stopped me, asking me to sit and wait. He indicated at the chairs which were fixed atop a long steel rod attached to the wall.

I didn't have any option than to sit. All the chairs were vacant. I sat on the second. I was breathing heavily. I closed my eyes. I have known her for five years. Back then we were classmates. “How beautiful and cute she looked at that time!” I was lost in the past. I was soon transported to the past through the eyes of my mind.

Chapter – 1
Let's go back some years

* * *

It was the first day at my new school and I was brimming with excitement. When starting something new, a general fright is the usual companion, yet my enthusiasm drove me on.

Our school bus stopped with a jerk in front of the school. I stepped down strapping my black bag on my shoulder. The school was splendid, with red tiled roofs and spotless white walls. In one look, I counted that there were sixteen yellow buses standing parallel to each other with the school's name M.K DAV was painted in bold red letters. That whole area was painted in white and grey which was also the colour scheme of our uniform - White shirt and grey trousers.

On entering the campus, I could see numerous students wandering here and there.

"Excuse me." I stopped a boy who was walking towards my direction.

"Where is class ninth." I had completed my previous education from another school called Gyan Niketan.

"There, in senior wing." He raised his hand and

indicated towards a huge identical building. "This is the junior wing" , he added.

Before I could thank him he rushed towards the senior wing, which he had mentioned earlier. I followed him and entered through a black gate that led into the ground with cemented flooring. At the left end of the ground was a giant stage and at the right side, a beautiful garden. Beyond the field, there was a three floored building with classrooms.

"Class ninth C?"I asked a boy. He didn't say anything but pointed at the top-floor with his forefinger.

I climbed up the stairs towards the first floor, guided by little boards stuck on top of every class-room door, indicating the name of the class. After passing four classes, I finally stood in front of the board that said "Yes I am class ninth C".

I entered the class. There was no one except for a boy who was walking out after keeping his bag on a desk. Colourful bags occupied the top of various desks.The owners of those bags were out in the corridor huddled in groups of three or four, chatting merrily.

"Hi!" I extended my hand towards the boy. "I am Manav; newly admitted."

"Oh! new admission? Ankit. My name is Ankit Jaiswal." he held my hand and said" Come.. Come here." He almost dragged me to the second bench of the first row. He pulled my bag off my shoulder and kept on the desk.

"You will sit here." His behavior was peculiar but I didn't think much about it and walked out of the class with him. Among many others like us, we leaned against the railing of the corridor and gazed down towards the ground. Some other students were sitting in the garden and chattering animatedly.

A long metallic bell broke our conversation.

"TAN... TAN.. TAN..." Students started gathering on the cemented landing in front of the stage.

"Let's go, the morning prayers will start now." Ankit said and moved towards the stairs. I followed him and placed myself right behind Ankit in a queue, on the cemented landing. Separate row for separate classes were formed by students for prayers every day.

The empty stage, I noticed, was now adorned with different musical instruments like the Harmonium and Tabla. behind which there was a student to play it. A choir made up of beautiful girls stood behind the mic.

"Attention" the head boy's voice boomed and echoed across the field. All the right legs rose up in the air and fell together on the ground producing a resonating 'KADAAP'.

"Commence Gayatri Mantra", he commanded and joined both his hands. The whole school followed him and assumed a prayer position. Students behind instruments started playing in a wonderful unison, and it seemed as if they were controlled by the same switch.

Five times we recited the 'Gayatri Mantra' which was followed by a pin drop silence.

"Commence the morning prayer"said the voice on the microphone again.

The Gaytari Mantra followed by the morning prayer was wonderfully accompanied by the music. My heart and soul felt peacefully refreshed.

Soon after, a person with a bearded face appeared on the stage. There was a wide smile on his face. He walked slowly and kept his right hand on the podium, adjusting the mic with his left hand. "Good Morning students." he wished.

"Good Morning sir" whole school echoed back.

"I am V.K Singh your principal." He introduced himself. He welcomed the new students and welcomed back the old ones. He wished everyone well, showering the morning assembly with words of gentle blessings and then spoke a few minutes about discipline, school, what our aim is and what the school expects from us.

I don't think even a handful of students were listening to him seriously. Everyone was waiting for him to finish his speech. At last he was done and we all were told to go to our respective classes.

Ankit and I entered the class along with the other boys but I froze where I stood when I realised that the row in which Ankit had placed my bag was all occupied by girls. The desk with my bag on it was vacant and the girls around the desk were probably expecting some new girl to come fill it.

I looked at Ankit. He was smiling. I understood that I had fallen victim to his prank. I looked this way and that and dragged my feet slowly towards the second desk. A girl was sitting on the bench right next to this one.

"That's my bag; actually I am new and", before I could complete my sentence, Ankit screamed "Sit there with *chawanni* (25 paise)." The whole class broke into laughter.

"SALLE! Is your mother's rate '*chawanni*' or your sisters'?" That girl flared up. She stood angrily at her place. I was so nervous, I did not even notice how beautiful she was at first. . She was stunning. She was the tallest and the most fair among all the girls in the class. Her skin was white as milk and the composition of her face was marvelous; straight nose, lovely lips and curly hair. Her eyes had a unique attraction about them, this was her most remarkable feature. Before I could bring myself to look at her eyes again, she growled. "KAMINA have you seen your face? You think yourself a hero? Even your height is less than mine and you are calling me a CHAWANNI?"

Really, Ankit was 2 or 3 inches shorter than her. I

didn't know what the history of CHAWANNI or their clash was so I stood confused and quiet looking alternately at her and Ankit. I was still standing in front of my bag considering whether or not to take it.

"They come from houses with no women" She grumbled as she sat down.

The girl was fuming and I considered it best to move as far away from her as possible. I picked up my bag and found Ankit nodding in my directing with a 'come here' expression. I was curious about the mystery of CHAWANNI and couldn't wait to ask him about it.

He scooted aside to give me place to sit. "Sit here." Ankit offered.

"Why was she abusing you?" I sat keeping my bag on the desk. "And what is this CHAWANNI?"

"Nothing *yaar*, don't bother" Ankit said.

"There must be something if she was abusing you like that." I pressed on to make him speak.

"Look, it's common here! Her nickname is CHAWANNI and she flares up like that anytime when someone calls her that." He chuckled.

"How did she get this name? She is tall and elegant then how does CHAWANNI make sense? "

"There is a long story behind that".

"Please tell me. I want to know" I urged.

"Nothing interesting, once Vishal proposed to her and.."

"Vishal who?" I interrupted

"See that boy who is sitting parallel to that girl?" He pointed secretively.

I saw. He looked fine with his average height, round face and a wheat-y complexion.

"What about him? He likes her?" I asked.

"Not only like that AASHIQ BOL" Screamed Sagar

who was third in our row.

"He is also a unique boy" Ankit started. "He always follows her and joins the same coaching classes where she goes but she doesn't even look at him."

"What happened to Vishal's proposal?" I tracked the conversation.

"She is arrogant about her beauty, she even complained to her mother."

"Direct to mom? Then?" I asked.

"Then what? Her mother came to the coaching centre in the evening and created a big scene."

"Why? What did she do? " I asked eagerly.

"Her mother is even more arrogant than her. She started scolding Vishal in front of the whole batch. She started yelling *What is your AUKAT, by looking at you I can very well judge you and your family.* and a lot more."

"Vishal didn't say anything?"I queried.

"At last, when she taunted that he is not worth even a single rupee, he lost his patience and said If you threaten my worth and my status, you should also note that it was I who your daughter any priority, else your whore daughter doesn't even deserve a CHAWANNI."

"CHAT" her mother slapped him. The whole batch echoed with oohhhs and aahhhs.

"What are you doing?" The teacher had come into action now. "How dare you slap him in my class? Better take your daughter with you."

"I am not interested in sending her here myself. " she tugged at her wrist and went off.

"And from that day, CHAWANI became her nick name." Ankit completed.

The whole class suddenly became quiet and attentive as a person of about thirty - thirty-five entered the class with an attendance register in his hand.

"This is Pandey sir, our class teacher" Ankit whispered.

He started calling out names.. He taught mathematics. After mathematics we attended three more boring lectures after which we had lunch.

During lunch all the students filled out of the class. I had to wash my hands and found my way to the wash basin. I saw the same tall girl was filling her water bottle there. Her water bottle was also cute like her. There were many little teddies printed on it.

"Sorry" I said and she raised her face and looked at me. "It's because of me that you had to go through that and" I wanted to justify but she interrupted.

"No, No Don't be sorry. It's not because of you. It's common. I never disturbed any one, never bothered in any one's work but I don't know why do they always target me? They love to tease me." Her voice contained more pain than complaint.

I didn't know how to respond. She guessed my hesitation and soon said, "leave it. I don't want to talk about them."

"What is your name?" How stupid was I? Ankit talked about her for an hour but I didn't bother to ask him her name.

"Naina", she looked at me with her big eyes. She had filled her bottle completely and was now tightening the cap of the bottle to close it.

"Nice name, it must be because of your big and attractive eyes. HAI NA?" I was still looking at her eyes.

"Don't know, but mom loves to call me that." Her fondness for her mother could be seen in her eyes. We moved back to the class.

"What is your name?" She asked me.

"Manav."

"Why are you solelyManav? Aren't we allManav?" she laughed.

"It's not like that." I joined in her laughter.

We reached our class. She turned towards the girls' side and I rushed towards my seat.

"KYA BAAT HAI! Sixer at the first ball" Ankit commented as I reached. I understood what he wanted to convey.

"Have you gone mad?" I took my lunch box out of my bag.

As I opened my lunch box, a jumble of hands reached in and all my food vanished in seconds. Same thing happened to Ankit. He was left with only one biscuit in hand. I kept my empty lunchbox in the bag and prepared for my loot. I scooped at Sagar's lunch box and got a piece of bread with some veggies. I don't remember if it was good or bad but it was fun to snatch each other's food.

After half an hour of the lunch break, we attended three more lectures and were soon off to our homes, shouting and screaming with joy in the bus.

Chapter – 2
Is It Love?

* * *

There was no teacher in the class. Pandey sir usually came late which gave students take the liberty to gossip and move around. Ankit stood with a notebook in his hand near the lecture desk. I bowled a folded paper ball which Ankit batted screaming "Six."

That little ball of crumpled paper few across the class and landed on Pandey sir who had just entered. The whole class went quiet in shock. I sat down noiselessly.

CHAT Ankit's face became red "Is this a playground?" Pandey sir growled.

"Sir .. I .."Ankit stammered.

"Go and sit at your place" he roared.

Eyes cast down, Ankit walked back to his seat. I scooted away to give him space to sit. I smiled at him. He glared at and asked. "What?"

"Nothing" I was laughing with my mouth covered.

"Asshole" He cursed.

I could hardly curb my laughter. Pandey sir started taking attendance. What followed was a long period of drab lectures.

We counted minutes throughout the day. The sound of the last bell felt like the sweetest harmony to our ears, it meant we could go home.

A week passed and a new girl was admitted in our class. Her name was Shipra Kaur, a Punjabi girl. Her hair reached down to her waist like old Bollywood actresses. She was fair and beautiful but not so strikingly so that could catch the attention of the class' boys. Like others, I too did not notice her all that much at first. But after a month she was the centre of everybody's attention as she became our house captain. She must have had some hidden talent.

Our school was divid-ed into four houses after the name of the four Vedas, namely – Rig house, Yajur house, Saam house, Atharva house. House captains for each of the houses were selected by our principal after an interview process. Those who wanted to be the house captain were required to fill the nomination form which was submitted to the principal and on an announced date, all the participants were interviewed and the house captains were declared the next day.

We couldn't be bothered even if our country elected a new President. then how could we bother about a new girl becoming the house captain? But one day she forced us to bother.

After the morning assembly, each class had to march back to their respective classrooms in a proper queue but Ankit, Sagar and I had the habit of walking parallelly with each other and chatting. The house captains had the duty to monitor the movement of the students at different locations. Shipra was standing on the stairs that day.

"Go properly in a queue." Shipra ordered.

We avoided her command and continued walking as we were.

To take orders from a girl would have bruised a

young boy's ego like mine in those days.

When we ignored her she tugged at my collar from the back back. "I told you to go in a queue, no?" she ordered.

Anger flashed through my mind. A girl had taken me by the collar, it was very insulting for me. All the other students gather ed around to enjoy the scene. I turned towards her and said "AGAR AESE MERA BAAP BOLE TO USKA BHI NA SUNE, TO TU KYA CHIZ HAI."(I would not even have taken my father's command, had he spoken to me like this, then who the hell are you?)

"Talk in English." she said.

"HA TU TO LONDON ME PAIDA HUI HAI NA?" (London-born, are you?) I continued. Hearing this, the boys around me laughed massaging my ego.

"You bastard, what do you think of yourself? I will" she started in loud voice but before she could complete I blurted out louder than her. "Quiet you, bitch!"Just then, Naina reached the scene..

"What is this Manav? What are you speaking?" she was not angry but her voice was loud. I didn't say anything but only looked at her. How beautiful she was! During this lapse in moment, Shipra got a chance to speak.

"What does he think of himself? He is abusing me. I will make a complain to the principal."

Naina looked at me. "She tugged at my collar" I told her as I believed I was innocent.

"You should leave." Naina told me.

"But "I tried to explain but she interrupted.

"Manav, please go", again she requested me.

"CHAL AB CHOR BHI" Ankit and Sagar insisted and I took the stairs leading up to the classroom. I knew there would be gossip about that incident in the class. After a few minutes, Naina and Shipra entered the class together. I didn't know what she told Shipra? How must she have convince her not to complain?

After Pandey sir's class we had Mathematics. My gaze randomly drifted to that Punjabi girl. She had pulled her pony tail to the front and in her lap and was playing with it. When she noticed that I was looking at her she flicked it back and sat straight. I shook my head and tried to concentrate on Pandey sir and his Algebra but my focus was weak and my eyes towards her again. She was rotating her pen with her fingers on the desk. She caught my glance again. She kept the pen aside and looked straight ahead towards the teacher. I smiled.

"Why are you smiling?" Ankit asked, confused. "Are you not copying the sum?"

I only nodded in affirmation and looked ahead at the board. I sneaked a look at her again and found her smacking her lips with the pen. She tried to snub me in front of the whole school and yet I was looking at her. If I wanted to look at somebody,

It should have been Naina. She was prettier than Shipra, yet my eyes searched for her. Why? I am not sure but I realised that I loved to look at her engage in stupid activities. She was fidgety and couldn't sit still even for two minutes. If her hair were shorter and untied like others, perhaps she would have looked more beautiful.

I kept thinking about her. Mr. Pandey's Algebra went over my head. Once again, our gazes met and I quickly averted my eyes once more time.. At the lunch hour, cute Naina was filling up her cute water bottle at the water taps.

"Hi" I said and turned the tap to wash my hand. She smiled in response.

"How did you convince her to not complain?"

"Forget it now, it's all over."

"Yes, madam" I bowed in front of her like a waiter.

She smiled her wide smile.

One evening, Ankit, Sagar and I were standing in front of a CHAT stall on Thana road with a plate of SAMOSA CHAT each. Thana road is famous for Daltonganj's best CHAT.

"See, that's Shipra there!" Ankit exclaimed.

"Where? "Sagar and I followed Ankit's gazennwhich went to a rickshaw carrying Shipra and a lady.

Perhaps she was her mother.

Our eyes met and we surrendered whatever was left of the 'samosa chaat' to the dustbin.

"Let's go" Ankit sat on the bike and kicked up the ignition. I was last one to sit. Sagar sat in between us. Ankit accelerated and we over took the rickshaw. I turned my head back to see her. Our eyes met for a second before she looked away.

"Slow. Slow." I patted on Ankit's shoulder. He de-accelerated the bike enough for us to come parallel to the rickshaw. Our eyes met again. Her mother could very well notice our shenanigans but we didn't care. Their rickshaw overtook us for a bit but Ankit roared up the accelerator and we found ourselves ahead, turning and looking back at her.

"Stay behind." I said.

We rode slow enough to just manage following Shipra's rikshaw. Three people on a bike with neither the helmets nor a license is punishable by law but in our city the rules were not so strict. We passed two traffic signals and reached in front of her house at 'BELWATIKA '.

"SASURAL TO MAST HAI BHAI" Sagar exclaimed looking at the two storied house.

It is often so that if a guy likes a girl, ,whether or not the girl feels the same for him, his friends derive premature relations; making her brother 'saala', her house 'sasuraal' and her father 'sasur ji'..

It became a habit for me to spend the whole day staring at her. She looked at me some times too from the corner of her eye. Whenever our eyes met I felt a pleasant sensation run through my body which made me ask myself "Am I in love?" The only answer I got each time was, "I don't know."

I didn't have any previous experience of love at fourteen. I did not have any memories and lessons to draw from. I did not know what people felt or did when they were in love.All I wanted was for her to be infant of my eyes at all times. I felt like there was a lot inside of my to tell her. I wanted to tell her the little things that I noticed about her everyday The little things that made me surge with emotion. How important and beautiful she was to me. I wanted to tell her a lot more but I didn't dare say a single word.

Why are we frightened to express ourselves to the one we love and suppress all our feelings inside, instead? Why don't we speak out? I think it's because of the fear of rejection. However, I feel one should express oneself once, either the person will yes 'yes' or 'no'.There is nothing more to it.

Even though I believed in this theory of mine, I didn't have enough courage to tell her about my feelings.

One evening, all three of us got on our bike again and reached the front of Shipra's house. She was standing on her balcony, looking stunning in her blue top.

Ankit sounded the bike's horn to catch her attention towards us. We looked at each other for a split second. The bike did not stop, we rode from in front of her house, and returned to take another lap from a little distance away. All this while the game of glances was had started to keep score. We repeated this about four times and had started to get noticed by her neighbors. A girl on the balcony and boys taking rounds on a bike below, this wasn't the most difficult riddle to crack, even for a child.

"It'll be best to leave now, people are staring at us." Ankit said and turned the bike around. I wanted to look at her some more but our situation was getting bleaker by the minute.

"ABE DARTE HAIN KYA? Let's go again." Sagar said unabashedly.

"MUJHE MAAR KHANE KA SHAUK NAHI HAI." Ankit said sarcastically.

Some girls are gifted thus, that they can accurately judge a man's gaze and decipher the expectations and intentions behind it. They understand everything, even if they decided not to express it.

Shipra might have known the reason why I always stared at her and might've guessed what I wanted from her but neither she did express anything, nor I.

Girls can easily hide their emotions and feelings even if they are in love they won't confess their entire life.

The next day, at lunch, Ankit was about to open his lunch box and we were standing around him, smiling ready to scoop. As the top was removed, all hands went towards the lunch without even see-ing what was in it. Before anyone else could, I picked up the lunch box and tried to run away, but as I turned back, I collided with someone. I raised my eyes and realised that it was Shipra. All that the lunch-box held, fell on her. It was then that we came to know what the lunch box held, it was noodles. There was a big yellow stain on her modesty . I was frightened that she will flare up.

"Sorry Sorry , I didn't see you. I will clean it." I raised my hand to wipe but she had taken two steps back. "Hey! What are you doing?" She blurted. Only when these words came out of her mouth, that I realized what was I going to do.

"Sorry, I really didn't mean to do that." I was really

nervous. My first love was in front of my eyes. If there was someone else instead of her, I wouldn't have reacted so foolishly but it was she whom I liked. For whom I felt 'SOMETHING LIKE LOVE'. It was she who always made my heart beat so fast.

"It's okay." she was patting away on the yellow spot hoping to remove it spot but in vain. Some bits of noodles which were stuck to her shirt fell down but that yellow spot was still there.

"Does it suit you to quarrel like animals for food?" She asked sarcastically but we ignored her question.

She was a girl, how could she understand the feelings of boys? How could she know the bliss in this snatching? We were happy that she didn't complaint. After lunch, it was Satish sir's class and his eyes caught the yellow stain on Shipra's shirt.

"Shipra, what has happened to your shirt?" Sir enquired.

"Sir, noodles fell on it when I opened my lunch box." She lied point blank. Sir also didn't ask any further about it but her lie compelled me to think some more. Why did she lie? Does she also like me? Was staring and taking rounds of her house working? I was questioning and answering myself. In this process, the whole day went by and we rushed towards our buses.

Naina was standing alone near her bus. I took quicker steps and reached parallel to her and said "Hi".

She looked up to me and "Hi! what's up?"

I had almost forgotten about her from the day I started seeing Shipra. I didn't like to stare at Naina anymore. I didn't have any urge to talk to her. Shipra made me forget my first friend 'Naina'.

"Nothing" I replied.

"What about Shipra?" She asked smiling.

"Nothing Yaar, What should there be?" I tried to ignore the topic.

"I am noticing you and your eyes very well, which are always in search of her." She let me know. I only smiled sheepishly but said nothing.

"You like her, no?" she again asked.

"May be?" I shrugged.

She smiled. We boarded our respective buses.

After having a lovely dinner that night, I lay on the bed. My eyes were shut but I could not sleep.

You can't sleep just by closing your yes. It takes some time and during this time, we think a lot.

Shipra had dominated my thoughts. I was talking to myself. "Does she love me? Perhaps yes? She has an interest in me. She always looked at me and did not complain either after I messed up her shirt in class. How can I know she loves me or not? Tomorrow I will confess to her about my feelings." I decided.

This decision helped me sleep. "What will I tell her tomor-row? Should I tell her directly or should I admire her beauty a bit and then express my feelings to her?" Thinking about all that, I slept.

Next day at school, all my courage disappeared when I saw her. I went quietly to my place. Took my bag off my shoulder and kept it on the desk. Shipra was sitting alone on her desk. There was no one in the class except for the two of us.

My mind started egging me, "you have decided to tell her, go and tell. What will she do? She will either say yes or no. Go and tell her."

"O.K I am going", I replied to myself and went towards her seat but I didn't dare to stop in front of her. I stepped directly out of the class. I saw Naina coming my way.

"Hi, Good morning." I wished her.

"Good morning." She smiled.

After keeping her bag in class she also came out and stood beside me holding the railing. Both of us looked down towards the field.

"Do you have her number?" I asked looking towards her.

"Whose? Shipra's?" She also looked towards me.

I nodded.

"Why are you going crazy for her? She is not even that beautiful."

Why did she say so? Perhaps, due to envy. I was not in the situation to investigate. "Please try, no? Please, for my sake." Tell her that I want her number.

"She won't give it." she said directly.

"At least ask once. Who knows, may be she will." I urged.

This had to be the answer to my confusion. If she would give her number, I would know that she likes me too.

"I am telling you don't indulge in all this." She tried to make me understand.

"Please try for my sake. You are my best friend, no?" I had sworn not to understand.

"REHNE DO, JAB KAAM HAI TOH BEST FRIEND." She said sarcastically.

"O.K .. O.K I will ask her." She finally agreed.

The warning bell to assemble in the ground for prayer broke our conversation and we rushed towards the morning assembly.

Chapter – 3

* * *

I came to the class to put my bag off and almost slammed it on the desk. I sat down taking a deep breath.

"What happened?" Ankit asked. He had come early that day.

"Splitting headache."

"Medicine?"

"Took it but it will take some time to come into effect."

I was annoyed because I was not willing to come to school but my mother forcefully sent me after giving the medicine.

"I can't go for the morning prayers today. You carry on. " I said

"CHORR NA, MAIN BHI JA KAR KYA UKHAD LUNGA?" Ankit shrugged and sat beside me.

When one is not feeling good, nothing in the surrounding can make you feel comfortable.

I rested my head on the desk in hope of some comfort.

All the other students had gone for the morning assembly. There was no one except for the two of us in the class. Ankit didn't have any work to do and was getting bored. He sat still for some time and then stepped towards the girl's row.

"Where are you going?" I lifted my head.

"Let's check the girls' bags." He said without looking back at me.

"Why? To steal food?" I sat straight.

"No, stupid."

"Then?" I enquired.

"Let's see they keep with them?"

"What do you mean?"

"Look, we keep sexy books and sexy photos with us. I want to know what kind of stuff are they up to?"

The idea seemed interesting to me so I went after him. My head-ache was now completely gone. Ankit opened a bag which contained nothing but a handkerchief and some photos of some girls. We found a photograph of a boy in Lata's bag.

"Boyfriend?" Ankit looked at me.

"Maybe." I shrugged.

For a while we found nothing interesting but we kept checking the other bags. There was a bag in red and black, Ankit opened the first chain and his hand brought out a blue plastic wrapper on which 'STAYFREE' was written.

"It seems her date is at hand." Ankit Laughed.

"Leave it, check what other things she has got." I didn't like to talk about a girl's private matters.

"Stop, I want to know how girls use it." He tore the cover.

"Are you nuts? What have you done?" I shouted. "She will come to know that someone has checked her bag. MARWA DIYA BE TUM TO."

He completely disregarded my protests. "See, girls use it like this." He kept that white napkin between his thighs.

"You are mentally sick. Do you know whose bag this is?" I asked.

"No, do you know?" He questioned in return.

I shook my head.

Only girls are blessed with menstruation on earth and Ankit was making fun of it. It is the greatest boon of nature, and we were punished for our activities soon enough.

The sound of the door opening startled us. Both of us turned to see Shipra standing there. She must also not be feeling well to have returned to the class in the middle of the morning assembly. She froze at the gate on seeing the white napkin between Ankit's thighs. He was stupid enough to not have removed it till then. He was in shock too.

"You opened my bag, you rascals!" She shouted angrily.

"Her bag! *SATYANASH*." We had not idea that it was her bag. Had this bag belonged to any other girl, I would have had a comeback ready but she.. my 'sweet heart'. I only looked at her blankly, unable to answer.

"How shameless are you? You are checking a girl's bag and picking out such things. How wicked are you?" She snapped. "Wait , wait I will show you who I am?" She went off like a gust of wind leaving us standing there dumbfound.

I recovered only after she left the class. "SALE AB TO FENK DE ISE." I snatched the napkin from in between Ankit's thighs and kept it in her bag. "What will happen now?" I looked at Ankit.

"Why did this bitch had to come just now? If she had come after some time, nothing would have happened." He was abusing her for his own mistake.

"Mind your tongue." I glared.

"SALE TUJHE PYAR KI PADI HAI? She will get us fucked. If the Principal gets to know about it, he will throw us out", he shouted.

He was right.

"What next?" I asked calmly.

"Just wait and watch what she is up to."

"Will she complain?" Hoping for any chance that she might not.

"Yup, she will. That is for sure, but what matters is who she complains to?" Ankit said dismissively.

Tension gripped us hard. We could not speak but only looked at each other's faces. We were waiting for Shipra like a goat waits for a butcher's knife.

My headache had vanished. I didn't know if it was the effect of the medicine or the situation.

After ten minutes she returned with Pandey sir, our class teacher.

"Oh! These heroes are here", he said sarcastically. "Come out both of you." He signalled with his forefinger. "This is what you do instead of attending the morning prayer?" He shouted angrily. "You go and sit." He patted Shipra's back.

She went to her seat and opened her bag. Whether she was checking for the napkin or assuring that there wasn't another theft, only God knew. I cannot tell what she found as we stepped out with Pandey sir just then.

"Sir, we didn't have poor intensions. We were looking through bags only for fun." Ankit tried to justify.

"You come here for fun? Checking a girl's bag is fun?" His voice was successively raising in pitch.

"Sorry sir, this will not happen again." We cringed.

"Shut up and follow me quietly." He ordered in a harsh voice.

He could have left us after scolding or punishing us with two or three slaps but no, he took us to the Principal.

The smiling man whom we had seen on the stage

on the first day of school was a totally different person from the one in front of us at present.

"I won't tolerate such bastards in my school. I want full discipline here." Principal sir snapped after Pandey sir told him of our sin in detail. "Suspend them for fifteen days."

Just beyond the principal's chamber, there was the administration block where our suspension letters were typed and handed over to us in an envelope. We were not allowed to attend classes that day either. Our suspension was effective immediately and were were sent home.

A suspension of fifteen days did not feel all that bad. We were not entirely studious so as to lament the loss of classes. What bothered us most was what excuse could we possibly give at home?"

We took our bags and walked out of the school.

"Now what? Home?" I asked Ankit.

"Never 'YAAR.'"

"Then?"

He shrugged "Let's see."

There was an aerodrome near our school. 'CHIYANKI AERODROME'. During election season, the aerodrome was used to receive helicopters. Prime Minister Narendra Modi used it to visit the town during the 2014 Lok Sabha elections for a rally. Otherwise, the aerodrome was used as a picnic spot. On Sundays the area was filled with families in search of some quality time. There were sparse hills on the far side of the aerodrome.

We walked through the black pitched floor of the aerodrome and reached the other side near the foot of the hills. There was no one there except for us that morning. Our school used to be in session from 6 AM to 1PM and it was only 7:30 yet. We decided to climb the hill.

Hills look smooth, green and beautiful from a distance but you don't find them quite so on reaching closer.

They tare full of rocks, big trees and lots of thorny bushes.

We managed to reach the top somehow and started looking for distractions to pass the rest of our school hours before we could head home. There was a big boulder under the shade of a tree. We took our bags off our shoulders sat on top of the stone.

"Look where we have ended up today due to your so called girlfriend." Ankit commented as soon as we sat on the boulder.

"HA SAALE, who was imitating the way girls use pads?" I asked sarcastically.

Then we started gossiping, chatting, laughing and mimicking anyone we could think of. We were talking nonsense to pass the time but it seemed like the clock was ticking even more slowly here. The time that flew by so easily at school seemed like it would never pass here. Every minute seemed like an hour.

As soon as our watches flashed 1PM, we rushed towards our respective homes. I tried to keep my behaviour usual like any other day. I hung my uniform in place, put off my shoes and socks, washed my hands and sat for lunch.

"School was good?" my mother asked habitually.

"Yes", I said without shifting my attention from the food.

How could she be told that I did not spend the day at school but on a hill. She didn't ask any more questions and got busy with her house work.

At 4 O'clock in evening, Ankit showed up and we left for our coaching class after picking up Sagar from his house. When we came out of the coaching, I told Ankit "Let's go there".

"Where? Shipra's? Never." Ankit blurted.

"For the blunder that you have committed earlier this morning, you'll find her standing there, ready to hit you" Sagar affirmed.

"Please YAAR!" I insisted.

"OKAY let's go!" Ankit kicked and ignited the bike's engine.

We found her standing on the terrace again. She was wearing a white t-shirt with a bright red heart printed on it. Our eyes met and she turned her head and spat out in disgust.

"Oh God! so much of hatred?" I closed my eyes. She stormed off in anger.

We returned without taking any more laps. I was quiet. Perhaps Ankit felt my inner turmoil. "I told you not to go", he said.

I didn't respond. We returned to our respective homes quietly.

After dinner, I twisted and turned in my bed. Sleep evaded me. The sight of her spitting flashed in my head again and again. Had my love story ended, even before starting? Perhaps she thought us loathsome because we had checked her bag? No, it might be because of the particular thing which we took out of the bag. What was my fault in that? That was Ankit's idea. She only saw me sitting with him. Should I tell her the truth? Should I apologize? I was regretting being Ankit's accomplice in checking girls' bags.

These thoughts turned over and over in my head till I drifted off to sleep.

As usual, the next morning, my mother shook me awake."Get ready for school." I opened my eyes.

School? What school? I couldn't go to school for fifteen days but how could I tell her about it? I had to pretend to go to school and I did exactly that. I got ready and reached the bus stop but instead of the bus, I took an auto and reached 'RED-MA CHOWK'.

I lived on 'PANKI ROAD' near 'REDMA CHOWK'.

One could go four ways from there. On the left, was our school; on the right, the way to 'BAIRIYA' and straight ahead was the district court.

Ankit was already there. I walked towards him.

"Hi. What's up?" I asked.

"Nothing much, just wondering where and how to spend the time today." He replied.

"Why don't we go to the same place?" I suggested.

"Yes, that is an option." He said. "Wait!" he turned and rushed towards a wine shop which was right behind us. It was the only shop that opened so early in the morning. The shop staff probably slept in the shop and opened it as soon as he got up.

Ankit told me to wait at a distance but I followed him anyway.

"Two beers." Ankit demanded at the couner.

"I don't drink." I informed him but he didn't bother to listen. He took the bottles and kept them in his school bag.

"Let's go now."

We reached the hill and sat on the same spot on the boulder under the tree. Ankit used his teeth to open the metallic lid on both the bottles. He pushed a bottle towards me. Water droplets condensed on the outer surface of the bottle indicating the chilled temperature of the beer.

"I don't drink, I already told you." I did not show any inclination towards holding the bottle.

"*ABE LE LE*" He urged.

"But I have never had this to drink before, how can I?" I hesitated but held that bottle.

"Taste it once, it will help you pass the time and you will feel like you are on cloud nine." He forced me.

"What about when I go home?" I was still hesitating.

"Its effect won't last that long?" After some hours

you will feel normal again. He tried to convince me.

It considered to try it once and took the bottle to my mouth. I took one sip and shut my eyes tightly. It tasted terribly bitter.

Ankit looked at me and threw a packet of wafers towards me. "This will help you. Go slow and take a bit of wafers after every sip." My first lesson in drinking came from him.

For the few initial sips, I struggled with the taste. It felt difficult to swallow the bitter liquid down my throat. As it started to come into effect, it got easier. It had tickled the pleasure cells of my brain and the taste didn't matter anymore. I continued to drink and eat. We started talking, talking a lot and talking crazy. We didn't even know, what words came out of our mouths.

Soon we were completely drunk. We had our empty bottles in hand.

Ankit stood on the boulder and flung his bottle far away.

"I will fling mine farther away from yours", my voice trembled in influence of alcohol.

I felt like on top of the world. I rose up. My foot was shak-ing. I took a few steps with my shaking leg and threw the bottle in the air. I don't know how far it went, but under the effect of alcohol I couldn't control my balance and fell down. In that drunken state, even the rough stony ground felt like the cozy bed I had back home. I didn't show any effort to help myself.

"Manav.. Manav.." Ankit shook me.

I blinked repeatedly and tried to focus on his face. It took me some time to realise where I was. I sat down. Everything around me seemed to be revolving around me; the stones, the trees, other hills and even Ankit.

"Ankit. Why are you moving round and round?" I

asked in a funny voice.

"No one is moving, just sit here" ,he made me to sit on the stone.

He was under control. The alcohol didn't affect him all that much. Perhaps because he used to drink.

"Do you know how much I love her?" Ankit neither said anything nor asked about whom I was talking. He only looked at me quietly. "ITNA" I spread both my hands in the air, to the extent that I could possibly spread them. I was not in my senses to filter my thoughts. I said exactly what I felt.

"And she spat at me, at ME?" I emphasized.

"Does she not realise, how much I love her? Doesn't she know that checking girls' bags was your idea and you are the bastard who took out her..." I didn't complete my sentence but started laughing. "HA- HA-HA. Her STAYFREE." I laughed again.

Ankit was quiet still.

"See! girls use it like this" I imitated what Ankit had done in class and we laughed aloud.

Ankit stood this time and held my arm. "Its okay, now sit. Sit here." He tried to make me climb and sit on the boulder but I did not move from the ground. He gave up and sat beside me.

"But she shouldn't have done that." The alcohol was making me circle around the same point over and over again. "I did nothing wrong, then why does she hate me Ankit? Will you tell her that I didn't do anything?" I held Ankit's face in both my hands.

"Yes, I will tell her." He patted my shoulder.

"Oh God! Listen to me", I lay down on the ground looking at the sky. "I love her", I yelled with full intensity. "I love Shipra."

"Quiet, be quiet", Ankit shouted irritatedly. "If someone hears you, they'll come as ask what we were upto here?"

"Ssss...h", I held my forefinger to my lips. Alcohol made me sleepy. My hand slid down slowly from lips and soon I was asleep.

Ankit didn't wake me up this time.

When I regained conscious, I felt dull and weak.

I had a slight headache. My throat was so parched, it felt like I had not had water for decades. For a second, I couldn't recall where I was and what had happened to me. Had I fallen down? Where was I?

Things started coming back to me slowly, flashing in my mind one after the other and last thing I remembered was that I was drinking. I sat up and looked around with my half opened eyes. My back hurt as I'd slept on a rocky surface. I looked at my watch and it was 1:15 P.M. already.

"Oh God! I slept for 5 hrs." I shook Ankit awake who was lying next to me. He woke up with a jerk.

"Its 1:15, we need to get home." I showed him my watch.

We stood up, tugged our shirts in and mend our hair with our fingers. The essence of alcohol had not left me completely. My head felt heavy and I was still sleepy.

There was a 'DHABA' called 'PANCHWATI PLAZA' just outside the aerodrome. We washed our faces there and rushed towards our homes.

At evening we went to Shipra's place again but she was not there at her balcony. She had probably noted the time when we usually took laps around her place and was deliberately not present to express her anger. Perhaps, she would never present herself there again.

We continued to go to the hill for a few days after that. One day, we decided to go for a movie. It was a very bad idea, but we only realized that later.

Daltonganj is a small town with no multiplexes.

There were a few single screen cinema halls which were often frequented by families.

We bought tickets for the morning show lasting form 9 AM to 12 AM and returned back home at our usual time.

I sat for lunch but something was different today. My mother did not bring me lunch, instead asked, "Are you coming from school?"

"Yes, of course", one part of my mind felt fear but the other as-sured me that there is no way that she could know about my secret adventures?

"Have you attended all the classes? Name the teachers who have taken the classes today." Papa asked.

I wondered what he was doing at home in the afternoon. He usually came home late at night, due to work. I knew for certain, something was terribly wrong.

"Pandey sir, Satish sir, Ajay…." I started reciting the usual routine but before I could complete, "'CHAT' my right cheek turned red as papa had slapped me hard. "See how comfortably he lies." he said.

I understood that they had found out about everything. I didn't have an option but to bow my head and listen to whatever they had to say.

"Thanks to that shopkeeper who informed us, 'NAHI TOH YE KABHI BATATA BHI NAHI'", my mother shouted.

The same shopkeeper that my mother was so thankful of, I was abusing under my breath from the depth of my heart.

After a full dose of scolding, I was given some food to eat, which I ate quietly fixing my gaze low. May mother continued still with her shouting but it didn't bother me because I had stopped paying attention to her.

At 4 'o'clock, I got ready for coaching.

"Go to Pandey sir after your first coaching." Papa ordered.

"But why? I am already going to Kamal sir for Maths" I protested.

"Do what you have been told to do," his voice was harsh. "He helped a lot and also requested Principal sir to cancel your suspension. He said that you will be secure and do good in his custody and the Principal agreed with him."

"But I don't agree!" I wanted to shout but I couldn't. Ankit arrived and I left with him.

I was tied to one more coaching. I hated all the coachings and studies. The suspension had been canceled, which meant I had to go to school. How wonderfully these four days had passed but the next day I had to attend school again.

After the first coaching, Ankit asked whether we wanted to go to Shipra's house.

"NO YAAR", I told him everything that had happened at home that afternoon and about the additional coaching with Pandey Sir.

Ankit was happy because he got to go back to school without facing any of the drama which had happened at my home. "Okay then, I will also come with you. Let's drop Sagar at his home." We looked at Sagar.

"I think my Maths is also very weak." he said dramatically while scrubbing his head; we laughed.

That's what friends are for, ready to stick with you through thick and thin. That day, all three of us headed towards Pandey Sir's coaching instead of going to Shipra's house.

As I entered the coaching, I felt like hugging my father tightly. Shipra was there, sitting on the first bench. I hadn't seen her for four days and I was missing her. I could now satiate the draught in my eyes that her absence had left.

I averted my gaze when she caught me staring. She looked pretty in a pair of blue jeans and white top. I understood then that she complained about us to Pandey Sir because she took coaching from him and he, too, willingly took a hard action against us for the same reason.

We settled down. "How kind is your father? He sent you here directly to trap this girl" Sagar smiled and Ankit and I laughed.

After the boring lecture, we walked out with a sigh of relief. We saw Shipra leaving with Shalu on her scooty. We got on our bike and started following them.

Shalu was our classmate. She had a fair complexion and a bespectacled round face.

Before crossing 'REDMA CHOWNK', we overtook them. I turned around to look at Shipra, but her gaze was elsewhere.

Shalu sped up her scooty and overtook us. Both of them looked behind as if to challenge us.

"Oh, challenge?" Ankit sat up straight and gripped the bike's handle tightly.

Before he could accelerate I kept my hand on his shoulder. He understood my sign and kept his bike slightly behind them at all times. We were pretending to try to win but let them be ahead.

Sometimes losing is more important than winning.

"This CHASMISH is good for me. She will drive and I will sit behind holding her waist like this", Sagar exclaimed and held Ankit's waist.

We smiled. We followed them till Shalu dropped Shipra at her house and returned.

From that day on, it became our routine to follow them after the coach-ing till they reached their house.

All my efforts to impress her and win her attention were going in vain. It had been one month since this game had started but she didn't grant me even one look. I started at her all day but she didn't give me even one mistaken glance in return.

I talked to Naina whenever I got the chance and it was always about Shipra. She refused to get her phone number for me because she didn't dare to ask for it after the bag opening incident. I didn't insist further, as I knew I was in a bad spot.

Chapter – 4
Game and Love

* * *

Only one month was left before the Mahatma Hansraj Aryan Tournament (MHRAT). The tournament was like the Olympics for all DAV schools to take part in. Our school started its preparation for it too. Students who were good sportsmen were free to practice during the morning assembly and after lunch. We were happy to skip the four boring lectures after lunch.

I was a club volleyball player and had also played at the interstate junior volleyball tournament. The certificates I received there, I had submitted to the school at the time of admission, so I was called for the volleyball tryouts.

12 of us were competing to make the team and all of us played so well, even the coach was finding it difficult to select the final eight. Finally when the names were called, Ankit and I had make the cut.

After boys, girls' tryouts were about to take place We stayed back, how could we miss the chance to see the girls play?

Their game was not up to the mark. Some of them played good but rest could not even take the ball properly on their hands, making it deviate in all directions.

"Is this how you are going to play at the MHRAT?" Coach Mishra shouted.

"Sir, we will improve." said the best one amongst them. "Only a month is left, when do you plan to improve?" "Sir, please." all the girls requested together.

"Okay. I will see your game after 20 days and then I will decide whether the girls team will go or not."

Girls accepted the condition happily.

The bus dropped me early at the school the next day. None of my team mates had reached, so I picked up a volleyball and started rotating it on the tip of my forefinger.

"BHAIYA", somebody called and I shifted my attention towards them, dropping the ball. I dabbed it twice and held it in my hand again.

"Yes?" I turned towards the girl. She was a member of the girls' volleyball team and stood a little distance away along with her team mates. She was fair and seemed to have very soft skin. She looked cute, especially when she called me 'BHAIYA.'

"It's our ball." she said in her sweet voice.

They were right, I hadn't picked it up from the sports room as one is supposed to and I was the only person there from my team so it was obviously their's.

I didn't make any effort to return the ball.

"So?" I asked.

"We have to play." another girl said.

"I want to play too." I said stubbornly.

"But how?" she wanted to say but I intervened.

"Do one thing, until my team mates arrive, make a circle around me. I will pass the ball to every girl."

It was their senior's order and they didn't have an option but to agree with whatever I commanded.

After some time, the sports teacher arrived. I held

the ball and wished him.

"Good Morning." he nodded. "You are doing the right thing, make them practice daily."

"No sir, my team has not arrived yet so I am playing with them. When my teammates come, I will go for my own practice" I protested.

"No, you play well and an hour of practice is enough for you, but these girls need rigorous practice to come up to the level of the tournament", he insisted.

"But sir…." I wanted to say something more but he interrupted.

"Don't argue with me now. The girls' team is your responsibility, prepare them for the tournament".

"Yes BHAIYA please! We need a coach." all the girls shouted.

"Okay, I will help you practice but I am not a coach. I am not that good." I said, tossing the ball to one of the girls.

After lunch we gathered in the ground again for practice. The boys went to their court but I stayed with the girls. I asked them to make a circle again and made them practice passing.

I passed the ball to the girl who had called me 'BHAIYA" that morning. She raised the ball in such a perfect arc that I couldn't resist myself from smashing. I smashed the ball at the same girl.

"Aaa..a", she yelped after attempting the ball. She sat down holding her hand.

I forgot about the ball and ran to her. "What happened? Are you okay?" I held her hand. The place where ball had hit had turned red.

"RUPU are you okay?" All the other girls had gathered around us.

"BHAIYA I am fine. It's okay." She stood twisting

her wrists. "I am not so weak", she smiled.

Due to her cute smile and the way she called me BHAIYA, I started feel-ing a brotherly affection towards her. She had all the qualities of an ideal sister.

"Hey! What is this RUPU?" I didn't start the game immediately.

"Her name is Rupali, but in short we call her RUPU." Shreya clarified.

"YE RUPU KATORE KATORE." I joked and all the other girls broke into laughter.

"BHAIYA don't distort my name." Rupali sulked.

"YE RUPU", I teased her again.

"BHAIYA!" she shouted.

"Okay, okay now we shall play" I clapped twice, "and no one will call her 'YE RUPU KATORE KATORE.'" We laughed again.

"BHAIYA" She stomped her feet and sulked audibly.

I tossed the ball at her, which she passed to another girl.

No one wanted to attend the lectures so other students started bunking classes with the excuse of sports too. Not just boys but girls too were participating in this bunking. To counter this, Ajay sir started collecting students present in the ground to point out those whose names were not present on the mailing list.

"The House Captain herself is bunking the class." I heard him say sarcastically.

Shipra had bunked the class for the first time but unfortunately she had got caught.

"Sir she is in the volleyball team." I tried to save her.

"But her name is not on the list." He waved the list at me.

"She joined after the team selection had taken

place." I clarified.

He turned his head towards our sports teacher. Mishra sir nodded. He understood me. He had a helping nature and always took the side go us sports kids. Whenever we had indulged in something or had done something wrong, we sought his shelter and he always tried his level best to save us. This time too he rushed towards the boy's court without asking me another question about the lie I told.

"Thanks" Shipra said, looking at me.

She had spoken to me for the first time. I didn't know how to respond. I only said, "It's okay."

For few seconds we only looking at each other without saying anything. When I recovered, I asked her to come play with us.

"Me? But how can I?" she hesitated. "I don't know how to play."

"Come no," I urged "no one is a national player here. We are also learning." I threw the ball gently at her which she attempted to hit with the closed fist of her right hand. The ball bounced away, instead of coming towards me.

"No, you need to make a fist with both your hands, like this." I held her fair and soft hands. A unique sensation ran through my body. I kept her left hand over her right, "attempt to hit the ball now using both your hands." I demonstrated.

She started playing like I had asked her to but she was too frightened of the ball. To make her get over her fright, I was continuously tossing the ball at her.

"BHAIYA! She is not even in the team." Rupali complained.

She didn't like the fact that I was wasting time on a girl who was not even in the team.

"Okay, take it." I threw the ball at Rupali and

signalled at Shipra to join the circle.

Because of this routine, we started growing closer. I had tried all kinds of ways to get her attention, like following her, staring at her and taking rounds of her house but she hadn't looked at me once, but volleyball made her start talking to me and taking interest in me.

Everyone was playing well learning how to pass the ball to each other. We decided to not let the ball touch the ground and we were doing pretty well. Shreya raised the ball at me and before I could bounce it to someone else, Shipra screamed "Manav, give it to me!".

It was the first time ever that she had demanded something from me. If she had demanded the moon from me at that time, I would have given my life to bring it to her. I tossed the ball at her. She stepped forward to take it but the ball slipped past her hand and fell on the ground.

"SHIT! you let the ball fall." Rupali screamed.

Shipra gave her a stern and nasty look. Rupali quieted down immediately as Shipra was her senior.

"Don't worry, we will try again." I took the ball in my hands.

Rupali didn't like the fact that I favored Shipra.

Shipra practiced daily with me but I didn't have the courage to ask for her number. I continued to follow her after the coaching. Due to volleyball and my involvement with Shipra, I completely forgot about Naina. I didn't have the time to think about her but whenever we saw each other we smiled or wished or waved at each other.

The girls were soon ready to practice on the net. The boring morning volleyball sessions suddenly became interesting and attractive as soon as girls came to court. All the boys gave their best to impress the girls and the girls improved their game while playing with us.

"Ankit" Shipra called out to Ankit as he was leaving

the ground after practice. I had left earlier that morning to submit the ball in the sports room.

"Yes, what happened?" Ankit asked confused.

"I want to talk to Manav", she said hesitantly.

"Why? What is the matter?" Ankit enquired.

"Nothing, *bus yuhin*."

"Then go and talk to him. What is the problem?" Ankit suggested.

"There is no problem but we have never talked before. How can I just go and talk to him directly?" she asked.

"As you talked to me. Just stop him and tell him whatever you want to tell him." Ankit said.

"No, please can you give me his number?"

"Yes of course, but I don't have my mobile with me right now and I don't remember his number. I'll tell him you asked me for it."

"Thanks, tell him to meet me tomorrow."

"What is the matter? Have you started liking him?" Ankit teased.

"No," she reacted immediately. "Just for friendship. I started playing volleyball because of him. I also feel very sorry for getting both of you suspended. I am apologizing to you now and tomorrow I will say sorry to him too."

"Shipra, checking girls bags was my idea. Manav had nothing to do with it." Ankit clarified.

Before Shipra could reply, I screamed for Ankit.

"Yes, coming."Ankit shouted back.

"Ok bye. See you around." Ankit told Shipra and ran towards me.

"Tell him to meet me." Shipra bellowed from behind.

"HARAMI BHABHI HAI TERI. What were you talking to her about?" I felt envious.

"She was asking for my number." Ankit said.

"Your number?" I asked with heavy sarcasm. "Have you seen your face?" Sagar started laughing.

"HARAMI, I was joking but you need to give us a treat."

"Treat? For what?"

"Give us a treat and I will set Shipra for you."

"You will set Shipra for me?" I asked sarcastically again. "Do you own her now?"

"Really I can do that." Ankit said.

"How?" I asked.

"First throw me a party, then I will tell you."

"Okay, but only Samosa." I surrendered.

"*KANJUS SALA*, something is better than nothing though." He agreed.

After 'SAMOSA' party he conveyed to me everything that Shipra had told him.

"SALA, you don't remember my number? You should have learnt it by heart." I spoke out my number to him.

The three of us laughed. This was delicious news for me. I wished I could dancing on the road. Suddenly, everything around me, the environment, the people started looking romantic and beautiful..

That night, I could not sleep due to the excitement of meeting Shipra the next day. I was thinking what to say to her tomorrow. How should I respond to her questions?

The next morning, I stopped Shipra while she was walking towards the volleyball court.

"Good morning." I wished her.

"Hey!" She turned back.

"How are you?" Words slipped out of my mouth, automatically.

"Fine. What about you?" She asked.

"I am good" I smiled.

The conversation halted for a dew seconds. Neither of us had anything more to say. We stole glances at each other and quickly shifted our gazes on being caught.

"So?" She broke the silence.

"So what?" I smiled sheepishly.

"Say something." She replied.

"You are very beautiful." I blurted out.

"I know." She Smiled. "You are also very smart".

"Really?" I asked but the truth was that I loved her compliment.

"Yes, and your game is even smarter."

"You are far too generous with your appreciation. You too will do better at your game very soon." I assured her.

"Let's see." I saw her priceless smile.

"BHAIYA! Won't you come? We need to start practice." Shreya screamed from the volleyball court. They were about to start the game.

"Yes, I am coming." I said cursing Shreya under my breath for interrupting our conversation. I looked at Shipra lovingly.

"Let's go," she said but didn't show any effort to move. I stood quietly.

"Shipra, we have a lot to talk. Why don't you give me your number." I said hesitantly.

"Yes, write." she started reciting her number.

"One minute please," I interrupted "I don't have a pen on me, do you have one?" Cell phone were not allowed inside the school.

"Yes, I do." she took out a pen from the pocket of her skirt.

I found out that day that skirts have pockets too. I wrote her number down on a rag of paper which I found lying on the floor.

A strange excitement ran through me.

Throughout the game, I felt a unique attraction towards her. I could feel the change that had come over me. I looked at her with a lot of affection called her name with a lot of fondness in my voice.

After returning from school, I changed my uniform, took my meal and then shut all the windows and doors of my room before calling her.

"Hello!" I heard a girl's voice. Her voice sounded a little different on the phone but I hardly had any difficulty in recognizing her. I didn't say anything.

"Hello! Who's this?" she spoke sweetly.

"Your lover." I said.

"Mind your tongue. Tell me who are you?" She asked harshly.

"Seriously, I died when I first looked at you." I curbed my laughter.

"Hello, you are Manav, no?"

"Manav? Who is Manav? I don't know any Manav".

"Manav don't be over-smart. I recognize you".

"Yes it's me." I laughed. "What are you doing?"

"Nothing. I was expecting your call." She replied.

"Tell me something".

"KYA BOLU? You tell me something."

"How are you able to speak? Is your mom not there?"

"No, I am in my room".

"Oh! Who else is in your family?"

"Mom, Papa and my younger sister 'Mona'. What about you?" she asked.

"Mummy, Papa and I." I said.

"Just the three of you?"

"No, I have my grandparents also but they live in

the village.

What about your grandparents?" I asked.

"They died when I was a child".

"Oh sorry." I said, unfeelingly.

"No, it's okay."

"So?" I asked.

"So what?"

"Nothing." I was talking to a girl for the first time and I was nervous. I didn't know or understand what to say.

"Have you seen the time? Don't you have coaching today?"

"Coaching?" I removed the cell phone from my ear and saw the time. It was almost 3 O' clock.

"Yes, I am going to get ready."

"Shipra, It was really nice talking to you and I want to talk more but this coaching…" I left the sentence incomplete.

"Same here. I liked talking to you very much but I have to leave now too."

"Yes, okay bye, see you there".

"Take care, bye." She hung up.

At the coaching, she looked at me very differently than before. I could sense a certain fondness in her eyes which I liked a lot. We were continuously looking at each other. After some time, I winked at her. She immediately averted her gaze and blushed. She turned towards the white board but her face was red.

After the class, we walked out and she crossed my path looking straight at me. She went to sit behind Shalu on her scooty and we followed after them. I asked Ankit to drive parallel to them. He hesitated as he had no idea of my conversations with her but our bike was soon parallel to their scooty.

"Hi! Looking nice." Shalu was confused as she didn't

under-stand to whom I was referring.

"Hi!" Shipra felt uncomfortable talking to me in front of all of us.

"Say thanks, I have complemented you." I smiled.

"Thanks" she said sheepishly.

"So, going home?" I asked.

"Yes, we are going to our homes but where are you all going?" Shalu asked before Shipra could reply.

"To your home," said Sagar, smiling. "After all we have been following you home for a month now. Don't you care?"

"We do, but why?" Shipra asked. Shalu turned for the SADIK CHOWK after crossing the over bridge. We lagged behind but Ankit took us parallel to them again.

"Because it's our duty to escort you safely to your home." Sagar said and laughed, followed by everyone else.

"We don't need you safety. We are enough for anyone alone." Shalu said.

We were about to reach to Shipra's house when I said, "Bye Shipra. Take care."

"Ok bye." Shalu stopped the scooty and we crossed ahead of them. After riding ahead for a few meters, we turned back, but by then Shalu had accelerated towards her house. When we crossed Shipra's house, we found a Punjabi man with white turban, aged between thirty to thirty five indicating us to stop. Ankit applied the brake with a quizzical expression.

"Which school are you all from?" that Punjabi man asked.

"D.A.V. Why?" I blurted.

"The same school as that girl? What is her name?" he asked. "WO KAUR JI KI BETI HAI USKA?"

We understood the reason for which we had been stopped.

"Uncle, it is not what you think." Ankit said.

"No, no I am have been observing you guys for many days now. You follow her everyday."

"No uncle, it's not like that. We came here for nothing."

"Is there a park here that you come daily to, for a change?"

"No uncle, I mean…" Ankit stammered.

"Quiet! From tomorrow I don't want to see you here." His voice was harsh.

We didn't have a choice but to leave. Ankit sped up the bike.

The next day, I told Shipra all that had happened.

"That must be Sharma uncle," she grimaced. "He is the secretary of our society. Now you will not come to my house."

"It's not fair".

"Please, he knows my father. If he tells my father, just think what could happen?" she looked frightened.

"Okay, but I will come up to 'SADIK CHOWK.'" "Is following me necessary?"

"Yes, of course. You are so nice that I don't want to part from you even for a second."

Like all the other girls, she loved flattery.

Chapter–5
Why did this happen to me ?

* * *

It was a warm summer evening and we were riding right behind Shalu's scooty, crossing the over bridge. The sun had vanished from the sky but the red hue still lingered, nostalgic of it's presence from a few moments ago. The evening breeze made the day pleasant after the 35 degrees hot afternoon.

Shipra stretched both her arms wide, like the wings of a bird. Ankit drove ahead so I was exactly parallel to her. I spread my arms too and touched the fingers of her right hand. She turned her head towards me. We looked at each other for a moment wordlessly. I took that as her consent and grabbed her fingers in mine. Ankit and Shalu looked us but continued to ride parallelly. I doubt if our small town, 'DALTONGANJ' had never witnessed such a romantic moment, when a girl on a scooty and a boy on a bike held hands and rode together. The people on the road started to look at us. When Shipra realized that she was being noticed by people, she tried to withdraw her hand but I held on to her more tightly.

"Manav, leave it! People are staring at us", she said

and tried to pull her hand back, but failed.

"Let them see. What is the problem?" I smiled.

"Manav, please." She pulled her hand back so strongly, that Ankit lost his balance. I immediately left her hand and Shalu sped ahead. Our unbalanced bike wobbled and wavered like a drunkard and at last fell down. We were not driving very fast thus prevented any major injury. Ankit had a minor cut on his hand. Sagar seemed unscratched. I didn't know if he was internally hurt. I had a cut on my forehead. We stood wiping our clothes. Ankit straightened his bike, cursing me and my love.

Shipra and Shalu came running towards us. Shipra stopped directly in front of me, "Are you okay? Your forehead is bleeding!". She stooped close to me. She put her hand on my shoulder and started wiping the blood on my face with her handkerchief. For the first time since I had known her, she touched me of her own will.

"I told you to leave my hand, didn't I? Why did you not let go sooner? I am sorry, you all fell because of me but it was really your fault, wasn't it?" she said in one breath. She stood so close to me that I felt her warm breath on my neck. I could smell the fragrance of her body and it was entrapping me. I looked into her eyes and she looking into mine. How deep and beautiful those eyes were! For a few seconds we were lost in each other and then without thinking I leaned in and placed my lips on hers. People around us who'd gathered because of our little accident exclaimed in shock. Till that day, no one had dared to kiss a girl on the road.

Shipra pushed me away gently. "What are you doing? People are staring!" she blushed. Her milky face turned red. She returned to Shalu's scooty without a word, her eyes cast down.

"SAALA, if you want to die, die alone." Ankit said annoyed.

"You got a kiss at least, but what about us?" Sagar supported him.

"Real friends don't demand. They only help their friends." I smiled.

"I don't need such 'HARAMI' friends like you." Sagar laughed and we also joined him.

I got excited just thinking that I had kissed my love and that too in the middle of the street, in front of the whole city.

* * *

The official letter for the boys team to participate in 'MHRAT' tournament was handed over to me by our sports teacher.

"BHAIYA, what is this?" Rupali enquired and took the letter from my hand.

"Permission letter for boys." I said.

"What about us?" she frowned.

"What can I say?" I shrugged.

"Sir!" She screamed as she saw the coach walking towards the senior wing and jogged towards him.

"Yes?" He stopped on seeing her coming towards him.

"Sir, are we not going to the tournament?" she asked.

"You all are playing very dull, what can I do?" He said.

"We have improved sir, you said you would consider our case after seeing our game. Please sir! we have practiced very hard. Please give us a chance." Rupali tried to convince him. By then, the other girls and I had also reached the scene and stood there surrounding the coach.

"Try next year. Let the boys go this time." He said.

"At least watch our game. Please sir", she insisted.

"Really Sir, they have improved. They are practicing with the boys." I intervened to support them.

"Okay, I will talk to the Principal. Go and practice now." He rushed towards the senior wing.

After half an hour, he returned to the court. All the girls crowded around him with hopeful eyes.

He had brought good news. There was still hope of their participation in the tournament.

Next day, after the morning assembly, the boys' and girls' team stood outside the volleyball court. Two teams were formed, each containing four girls and two boys. The game started. The girls had practiced with us before and were comfortable and played well. The Principal was pleased with their game and finally allowed them to participate in the tournament. The girls were ecstatic. They rushed towards me and said, "BHAIYA we owe this one to you. We are very happy that you helped us improve our game."

"The credit goes to your effort alone and I am sure that you will be the winner of this tournament."

The tournaments were to be held at S.S D.A.V. in Delhi and we had to take a train there, the next week. Our school had hosted the tournaments the previous year and were the eight-years standing champion at Kho-Kho.

On the day of departure, I was the second to reach the railway station. Ankit was already there in a grey track suit with the name of our school written on it in white. It was our sports kit and we were strictly directed to be in it.

Shipra made me wait till the very end. I sighed in relief only when I saw her approaching at the railway station. She looked beautiful in the grey track suit. I saw her hair untied for the first time that day.

I loved the stray wisp of hair that fell across her forehead which she caught between her fingers and tucked behind her ear. She came and stood right in front of me but I was lost.

"Hey! What are you looking at?" She waved her hand in front of my face.

"You are beautiful." I blurted.

"Really?" She smiled.

I could die a hundred times to see her smiling like that. Right then we heard the announcement for our train that was going to arrive shortly.

The passengers who were sitting lazily, immediately got alert and rushed towards their luggage. After a few minutes, the train arrived on the track with a loud blow of the horn. We boarded the train and went to our respective berths. Shipra was with the other girls in another compartment so I left my place and passed through their unit, on the pretext of going to the washroom, just to get a glimpse of her. I did the drill twice and each time she looked at me with a cute smile. When I left my seat for the third time, Mishra sir said, "Why don't you go and sit with Shipra?"

"It's not what you think, sir." I felt as if I had been caught naked.

"*TU SHIPRA KE CHAKKAR ME HAI. YE BAAT PURA SCHOOL JANTA HAI.* (You are after Shipra, the whole school knows this.)"

I sat down quietly and didn't dare to stand again even when I genuinely had to go to the toilet.

The next day at 10:00 A.M, we de-boarded at the New Delhi railway station. We had a cab waiting for us which took us to S.S D.A.V. Their building was of the same colour but the architecture was far smarter and the campus much bigger.

We were allotted our respective rooms and I got separated from Shipra again. The boys and the girls were accommodated at separate places. Mishra sir instructed us to take rest as we had to practice in the evening.

I thought of Shipra, lying on the bed. "She is still unaware of my feelings. Will I have to tell her everything explicitly? Can't she figure anything out for herself? Can't she understand why I look at her all the time? Why I always find ways to be with her? Can't she think like me? Can't she feel like me?"

I kept thinking to myself, "What if she doesn't feel the same for me? What if she loves someone else? No that can't be. She has never mentioned anyone else, but then I have never asked her either. Should I ask her what she feels? What if she rejects me? No, she can't. I see love in her eyes for me but what if she doesn't want anything beyond friendship? I have to clear all these things with her. I have to ask her. I will express my feelings to her after this tournament is over." I decided.

These thoughts kept me awake for a long time and I overslept the next morning. Ankit shook me awake and I saw that my whole team was ready to leave. Ankit was also ready in his trainers. I yawned and said, "You people go, I will join you in a bit."

I sat up and looked around for the next few minutes. You generally feel dull right after waking up.

I reached the ground late. There were five volleyball courts, one after another. Both the girls' and the boys' teams were practicing together on court number 2 but Shipra was not there. I looked around for her and when my eyes finally found who they were looking for, pangs of envy burned my heart. She was playing with a tall boy at the left corner of the ground. He was fair and good looking. His hair reached down to his neck. One look and you could tell that he was a stylish and rich kid. Instead of going to the court I walked directly towards them.

"What are you doing here?" I asked Shipra.

"Nothing. Meet Pratap, Captain of the S.S D.A.V volleyball team."

"Hello," I gave him a curt handshake.

"In his captaincy, S.S D.A.V has won the last two national D.A.V Championships." She looked very happy with her new friend.

"Oh! Congratulations." I didn't like how she was praising him but I was helpless. "Don't you want to practice?" I asked her.

"I am practicing here. Where else can I get such an experienced coach?"

She was right. Where else could she get a coach like him? There was a day when she didn't even know how to raise the ball properly and now she was being choose-y about a coach. She had forgotten that I had given her undivided attention and coaching in order to get her there.

I turned back towards our court. I heard Pratap saying, "Do you have a boyfriend?"

She replied, "Not yet."

I reached to our court distraught, slightly angry and hurt.

"RUPU!" I called Rupali, who was standing at the service end to serve the ball.

"Yes BHAIYA?" She approached.

"Go and call Shipra."

"Why? What happened?" She asked.

"Nothing. Go and tell her that if she wants to play with M.K D.A.V, She has to practice with us."

She didn't ask any more questions and jogged towards them. She might have understood my feelings.

Rupali returned with Shipra by her side in a few minutes. I didn't say anything but signalled them to take their positions. No one uttered a single word throughout the duration of three games of 15 points each. The atmosphere was tense. They knew I was in a bad mood.

We took a 15 minute break then and I went to sit with Ankit, wiping my sweat.

"Manav" Shipra called me away.

"What happened?" I went towards her.

"You should not make an issue of my friendship with Pratap."

"I am not making any issue." I avoided looking directly at her.

"So what if I talked to him? I am saying something to you, look at me." She said.

"No need" I sulked.

"Okay, fine," She sounded annoyed. "I don't understand what the big deal is if I talk to him? He is also a friend, like you."

"Am I only a friend to you?" I looked at her for the first time then. I didn't like being compared to Pratap.

"Of course, you are only my friend. Is there anything more?" She asked directly, as if there was nothing beyond friendship between us.

I was speechless. I managed to hide my tears somehow. I loved her more than anything, but in return I got this. I couldn't believe it.

"Break time is over. Let's go practice." I said, fighting back tears.

I was not interested in playing any more. My attention was elsewhere. Really she didn't have any feelings for me? Was I only her friend? Had I lost her? Did I ever have her? Did she like Pratap? No, she never said that either. She said that Pratap was her friend. Perhaps she likes me but is not accepting it. After this tournament, there will be no Pratap in her life; then I will tell her how much I love her. She must accept me. But what if she doesn't? I couldn't imagine her rejecting my proposal. How could I?

Due to this inner turmoil, I played the worst game of my life that day during practice.

We returned to our cabin after practice.

The next day, Mishra sir displayed the chart of tournament games with fixtures. The knockouts were scheduled for that day. If we lost a single match, we would have to pack our bags and return home.

Coincidentally, our first match was with S.S D.A.V and the girls' team got D.A.V KAPILDEV as their first rival.

"Girls are standing already on the ground you all also reach there." Mishra sir informed us and left.

When I reached the ground, I saw that Shipra was talking to Pratap, but as soon as she saw me, she moved away towards the court. I didn't say anything.

Our game was better that day. Girls were playing well too. Shipra made a mistake once and I couldn't stop myself from remarking aloud, "This is what you have learnt from your new coach?"

"Manav, there is no need to comment."

The only thing pulsating in my mind was that I had to win the knockout game to impress Shipra.

When I was returning from the morning practice, I heard Pratap's friends saying, "Has she given you her number?"

"Yes. She texted me too." Pratap replied.

I knew that they were deliberately talking like this to make me hear.

"Have you given your mobile number to Pratap?" I asked Shipra when I caught her on the stairs.

"NAHI TOH. Why? Did anyone say anything?"

I knew she was lying. "Nothing", I said and stepped upward.

We put on our tournament kits and reached the ground. The court was beautifully adorned and marked with white powder. Before stepping into the court I bowed down to touch the ground and then took the dusty fingers to my forehead. I prayed to the almighty for help. S.S D.A.V won the chance to serve. The referee instructed the rules and structure of the game. We had to play three sets with fifteen points.

I stood at the centre, broke the service by S.S D.A.V and passed the ball to our raiser, Ankit. He raised the ball beautifully and Vinit finished it with a killer smash. Our opponents were taken by surprise and the ball fell to the left corner of the court.

Both the teams were equally balanced. After a difficult fight we managed to win the first round. We were drenched in sweat. Girls crowded the edge of the court and cheered our first victory.

"BHAIYA keep it up!" Rupali handed me an energy drink.

"We are going to win this." Prachi said enthusiastically.

"Manav, our school must win this match. Show them what we are!", shouted Shipra from behind.

Winning the game was important for me but when Shipra said it, it became absolutely necessary.

We resumed our game after the timeout. Shipra didn't talk to Pratap at all that day. She was cheering for me and my team and I loved it. I wanted to win the tournament and present her the match trophy.

The struggle resumed with the next round. Both the teams were strong and it was very difficult to score even a single point. Pratap was a good player and a nice captain.

We could not respond to his smashes.

The teams played neck to neck with thirteen points each. Had we scored two points more earlier, we would have won that match as we were already leading by 1-0. I was at the smasher position and it was our chance to serve. Pratap jumped to smash the ball again but I jumped at the same time and blocked it. The ball touched the ground on their side. The move was greeted by a loud applause and cheer from our supporters in the field. Shipra looked most beautiful enthusiastically cheering for me.

Chandu served the ball again and Pratap was ready for another smash. In an attempt to block, I jumped too but was a few seconds late in my response. The ball hit hard on the tip of my fingers and I fell to the ground clutching my hand. The score board showed that we had tied again. I looked at my hand and it had begun to swell. I cringed in pain. Mishra sir and the medical team arrived immediately next to me. They put a numbing spray on the wound and rushed me to the hospital. After an x-ray, I was told that my middle finger had a hair-line fracture.

I was discharged in the evening with my whole palm plastered. When I reached the school, the girls were about to start their first match. All the boys stood around to cheer them. When they saw me, everybody ran towards me.

"BHAIYA what is this?" Rupali asked.

"Nothing, only a hair-line fracture in my finger." I said nonchalantly. "Ankit, what about the match? Won?"

He shook his head sadly.

My heart sank."You couldn't even save a single set?"

No one said anything. I figured what must have happened there. After seeing my condition, Pratap's smashes must have frightened them. I felt helpless. We had lost the first knockout itself and were no longer in the race. I didn't want to leave with Shipra still there. I didn't want to give Shipra and Pratap the time and room to indulge with each other. The girl's team had to lose their first match if we were to go home together, which I did not want because I had worked very hard to get them here.

"BHAIYA, we are going to play now!" said Rupali.

"You go and take rest." Mishra sir told me.

"No sir, I want to see their match." I insisted.

"Thank you, BHAIYA." Prachi chirped. "Your presence will encourage us."

Shipra walked to me then. "Are you okay?" she asked.

"Yeah, I am fine." I replied. I appreciated her care for me.

The match started and our team dominated the opponents from the very beginning.They stood dumbfounded while Rupali smashed the ball left, right and centre. Prachi, Rupali and Shreya together were a force to recon with. They won the match with zero points against them. Two successful sets and the girls were shouting and jumping in celebration.

Rupali was the first to come running to me, "We have done it BHAIYA. Thank you, without your help it would have been impossible." The glimmer of happiness was clear on her face.

All the other team members came one by one to me and I con-gratulated them and shook their hands.

Shipra was the last to arrive. "You are my sweetheart Manav, because of you I played here and won."

Shipra had done a great job in the third line. She attempted and lifted all the smashes. I was happy because she was happy. 'Sweet-heart' was the sweetest word I had ever heard in my life till then.

"Congrats" I took her hand. How soft her hand was! A pleasant sensation ran through my body. How could she play volleyball with such soft hands? She withdrew her hand and turned to go. I didn't want to leave her hand but had to. I looked at her stockings and the swaying movement of her waist. A part of her fair thighs was visible right above her knees and below the hemline of her shorts. I started feeling aroused but averted my gaze immediately out of embarrassment. I loved her, how could I let myself think of her that way? It was wicked.

That night, we had a train back to Daltonganj and the girls came to see us off. Rupali wrote "Get well soon" on my plaster.

"Write smaller. We want to scribble too." Shreya exclaimed.

Everyone took their turns. Shipra wrote 'You won'. What had I won? The match or her?

Ankit took the marker in his hand and wrote on my plastered palm "SAALE DHOYEGA KAISE?" (How will you wash your rear after shitting?)

Everyone laughed.

"Idiot" I cursed him.

Upon reaching Daltonganj, I entered my house with the bag in my right hand.

"What is this? What happened to your hand?" My mother cried out and held my plastered hand.

"Nothing. Only a hair-line fracture".

"How did this happen?" Papa entered the room just then.

"While playing, the fingers bent a little too far. " I replied easily.

"I told you not to go. Now sit at home, handicapped." my mother yelled.

"Mom, it's minor injury."

"Minor? Had anything more serious happened to

you, would the school be able to reverse it?"

"It's okay, now please don't shout." papa calmed her down.

"You please be quiet, it's all your fault. I told him not to go but you supported him. Now he is back with a broken finger. Who is responsible?" Mom snapped.

Papa went outside. He didn't want to create a scene.

"These schools are totally rubbish. Instead of study they are only engaged in all this drama." In the eyes of a mother, her child is always right and innocent.

"Mom, give me something to eat. I am hungry." I tried to distract her.

"Go ask your school to feed you. You have broken your hand for them". She was undeterred. "From today, you are not going to play."

I was incapable of wiping my own ass, how could I play? I smiled remembering what Ankit wrote. My mother lectured me the whole day.

The girls were still back in Delhi and were playing surprisingly well. They had won the quarter final and were getting ready for the semifinals the next day. Shipra and Rupali kept me updated.

On coming back from school the next day, I dialled Shipra's number. She rejected my call. I redialed and the call got rejected again.

After a few rounds of rejection, I called Rupali.

"Hello BHAIYA." She answered.

"Hello! How is your preparation?"

"It's good, BHAIYA."

"Bang them in the semifinals." I told her.

"Sure, BHAIYA." She replied.

"Rupali where is Shipra? She is not taking my call." I enquired.

"Why are you wasting your time on her? She is not

your type."

"You know that I love her. Tell me where she is?" I insisted.

"I know, that's why I am telling you."

"Please tell me." I knew something was wrong.

"She has gone to watch a movie with Pratap."

"What?" I couldn't believe my ears. "How do you know?"

"I heard them talking about it. Please don't bother her. I am telling, you she is not your type." She stressed.

I hung up quietly. She must have understood my disappointment and didn't call me back. How could Shipra do this to me? I didn't try to resist my tears this time and they rolled down my cheeks. I was weeping for a girl for the first time in my life. "I am such a coward to cry like this for a girl. No! I am strong. I will not cry." I thought but the tears didn't stop. I felt as is someone was squeezing my heart.

That night I called Shipra again.

"Hello!" She picked up the call this time.

"Why were you not taking my calls in the evening?" I asked gently.

"The phone was on charge and I was outside." She lied.

"Don't lie. Had you not gone to a movie with Pratap?"

She didn't say anything.

"What happened? Tell me?" I broke the silence.

"Yes, I had gone to a movie with Pratap." She accepted.

"Why?" I asked.

"Why do you care? It's my personal matter."

"Do you love him?" I came directly to the point.

"Have you gone mad?" She screamed. "He is just my friend, and not even a good friend like you."

"So?"

"So what? I wanted to see 'CHAK DE INDIA'! You know already that Shahrukh Khan is my favourite actor. Three girls from S.S D.A.V were also with us. It was not a date!" She said loudly.

Her words comforted me. "Shipra I really want to tell you something."

"Talk to you later. I am going for dinner." She hung up.

My fate was against me.

For the first time in the history of M.K D.A.V, the girl's team had qualified to play the finals. The Principal, along with few teachers, had gone to watch the game and support the team.

"There was a day when the girls' team was not even allowed to participate in the tournament. They were told to prove them selves and now Principal sir himself has gone to see their match." I thought.

I was in the class but my mind was occupied with thoughts of the match taking place in Delhi.

It was Ajay sir's class. Numerical physics was going over my head. Just then a teacher appeared at the door and called for attention.

"Excuse me sir, I am here to inform you that the girls' volleyball team has won the final match at M.H.R.A.T" he grinned widely.

The whole class, including me hooted in unison, "Woo..., yes."

Ajay sir gave us a stern look.

"Why are you shouting? You lost your first match.

Have some shame." He was always too serious for his own good. I doubted if he ever laughed in his life. We quieted down with bowed heads.

The next day, the victorious girls' volleyball team

arrived at the school with the tournament trophy in their hands.

"BHAIYA one click with you please!" Prachi chirped and gave her mobile to Shreya.

"Of course, but how did you manage to bring your mobile to school?" I said surprised. The whole team stood around me.

"We have taken special permission from principal sir." Prachi declared. We clicked a lot of pictures, some even with the trophy in my hand. I asked Shipra to take some pictures with me, and she happily obliged. I sneaked my hand upon her shoulder. I was very happy that day.

"Prachi, please upload these pics on Facebook and tag me. I will download it from there." I said.

"Especially the pictures with Shipra Di. Right?" Rupali asked sarcastically.

"All the pictures." I said.

They laughed. Shipra also smiled sheepishly.

During the morning assembly, the captain of volleyball team was presented with accoladed and was asked to share her experience.

She took the mic in her hand and expressed how exhilarated she felt to be part of that team. She thanked her fortune for the victory under her leadership. She thanked the Almighty first and then her team, along with the Principal and the sports' teacher. She recounted how her team was ignored in the first place and how I supported and worked with them to raise their competency. She bestowed all the credit to me and her team and invited me to the stage so she could hand over the trophy to me.

There is a popular proverb that "Dogs can't digest ghee." I did not know how to digest all the attention and respect? I was taken by surprise and then stage-fright hit me. I had never stood in front of the assembly before.

My legs were shaking. My chest felt heave and it felt like no words would come out of my mouth. It was far easy to make noise below the stage and hide in the anonymity of the crowd, while being on-stage and deliver a message was a whole different thing.

"She has given me more credit than I deserve," I forgot to greet the audience. "It's the efforts and hard work of the team that has won them the trophy." I took a pause and started again. "They were good from the beginning. They had the capability to win and they did it." I didn't know what more to say and ended with a 'Thank you' and left.

I breathed a sigh of relief on coming down the stage.

"You spoke well." Ankit and Sagar told me.

"SALLE UPAR FAT GYA THA MERA." I said annoyed.

That evening I downloaded all the images from earlier that day. I looked at Shipra's pictures for hours.

A week had passed after the final match and Pratap's name did not come up even once. He was not there in Shipra's life anymore to make me jealous and uncomfortable. During lunch one day, Rupali and Prachi came to me.

"BHAIYA, today is Shreya's birthday." Prachi bellowed.

"Really? Happy Birthday!." I wished her.

"BHAIYA! We are bunking school after lunch for a treat and we are here to invite you."

"Are you instructing me to bunk classes?" I frowned.

"BHAIYA don't over-react. We know how attentive you are in your class." They laughed.

"Is this how juniors should talk to me now?" I joined in their laughter.

"I am not bunking alone. Ankit must be with us. I have done all my mischiefs with him." I smiled.

Shipra was absent from class that day and the proposal to bunk school seemed like a blessing in disguise.

"We have told Ankit BHAIYA already. He is ready to come with us but on the condition that you will be there too. Don't you two do anything alone?" Rupali asked.

"Never. We are one." I said with pride.

We entrusted the responsibility of our bags with Sagar. He was too serious to bunk a single class.

The five of us sneaked around to the building's rear end where the boundary was low and the area hidden from surveillance. One-by-one we jumped out and fled the scene.

"Where are we going?" I asked as we were out of the sight of the school.

"Let's go to 'LAZEEZ'" Shreya suggested.

"I am not going to travel so far." Ankit protested.

'Lazeez' restaurant was situated in a market area far from our school.

Why don't we go to 'Red Apple'? It is at a walking distance from here." He suggested.

"Yes, it's good." Everyone agreed.

When we reached the restaurant, I froze at the door. My legs refused to move and my heart sank. Shipra and Pratap sat occupying a table at the far left corner. Ankit and the girls stopped behind me. The birthday celebration and turned into a funeral. Shipra and Pratap stood as soon as they saw us. We rushed towards them and exchanged greetings. I was obviously gutted while shaking hands with Pratap.

"See, Pratap came here all the way from Delhi to meet me." Shipra said excitedly.

"Shipra I want to tell you something." Pratap said. "I have travelled all this distance only to tell you one thing. I want your friends to witness this too."

Shipra looked ecstatic. I knew what was coming.

The energy in the atmosphere made it obvious.

"Shipra," He looked straight into her eyes. "From the moment I saw you, I lost all control over my senses. I don't know why my heart starts to beat faster when I think of you. I close my eyes and I see your face in front of me. I wish to shout your name from the top of the world.

The fragrance of your body is in my soul. I can think about you for hours. I love the way you talk, you laughter, the way you play with your hair. I love everything you do."

Anger boiled in me with each word that he spoke. My palms itched to slap him right there. I couldn't say these things to Shipra even in moments of privacy and this bastard was declaring his love in front of the whole restaurant. Shipra looked very happy, and looked at Pratap unblinkingly.

Pratap went down on his knee and took out a single rose from God knows where. He must have kept it in his pocket or behind his shirt.

"Shipra, I love you. I love you from the bottom of my heart." He said.

It felt like someone had poured boiling oil into my eyes. Shipra blushed and smiled as if she had won some kind of a treasure.

"I was eagerly waiting to hear these words from you. What took you so long?" She took the rose from his hand. Pratap then stood up and hugged her.

I felt a wave of longing and desperation of an intensity that I had never experienced before. It felt like someone had taken my heart into their fist and squished it. I fought back bitter tears.

"I..I am..", I choked on my words. Tears leaked out of my eyes and I ran towards the door.

"What happened?" Shipra enquired.

"Nothing. He is not feeling well. We will handle

him." Ankit said.

"We will come with you." Shipra said.

"No, no. We will manage. You don't ruin your moment." Ankit said and came out.

Rupali was the first to reach me.

"What is this BHAIYA? Are you crying?" She kept her hand on my shoulder.

The lump in my throat got bigger and more painful. No words came out of my mouth, only tears ran down my cheeks.

"I will handle him." Ankit asked the girls to leave. They walked away silently.

Ankit and I went to the same hill-top where we used to go for drinking. I sat on my stone and closed my eyes. Ankit stood in front of me.

For the first half an hour, we said nothing. I couldn't stop weeping. "Why did Shipra do this to me? Why didn't she respect my feelings? Why does she need someone else? Hadn't I loved her? Why had she gone to Pratap? For the first time I had loved someone more than myself, but she loved someone else. I had lost my love. My first love remained incomplete."

Ankit left me to my tears. He didn't say a single word to console me. Perhaps he hoped that my tears will wash away my sorrow and anguish.

When I grew tired of weeping, I expressed my wish to drink.

"It is not possible." He said.

"Why?"

"Look at the time. We have to return now. School is over."Ankit showed me his watch.

I washed my face and returned home.

"Are you okay?" my mother asked upon seeing my pale face.

"Yes, why?" My voice was weak.

"You look sick. Your face is ashen. What happened?"

How do mothers know everything about their children? I couldn't hide anything from her. My eyes and expressions al-ways betrayed me to her. I didn't respond and sat for lunch.

When I was eating, she stood next to me and started patting my hair. "Don't worry everything will be fine", she said. Her love broke the barrier of my tears again.

"What happened? Why are you crying?" She said surprised by my sudden reaction.

"Headache." I couldn't tell her the truth.

"Sleep for some time. You must be tired."

She put my head in her lap and massaged my head. I felt a little calm and dozed off in her lap.

There is only one woman in this world who will never be-tray you. There is only one lap where you can rest anytime. For her, your happiness is always the priority.

It was already dark when I woke up. My mother informed me that Ankit had come to the house in the evening but she had told him that I was not feeling well and wouldn't go to coaching that day. I genuinely didn't want to go to coaching that day for the fear of seeing Shipra there. Seeing her face would have been like rubbing salt on my wound.

I saw her at school the next day. She looked pretty but I couldn't face her. Our eyes met for a brief second but I averted my gaze quickly.

I sat still and quiet in the middle of the chaotic classroom. I couldn't take my mind off the incidents from the past few days. A'good morning' broke the chain of thoughts.

It was Naina, the cutest girl in the world, and I hadn't talked to her for months. I had enveloped myself with the thoughts of Shipra and had completely ignored Naina in the process. That day she saw me sitting alone and came to say hello.

"Good morning", I tried to pull a smile on my face.

"You are sitting alone. Where is Shipra or has something happened between you two?" She touched a nerve.

"It's nothing", I shook my head. Just then the bell rang and I was saved from answering her.

During lunch, Shipra called me out from the class.

"What is it?" I managed somehow to smile.

She was looking straight into my eyes. I looked away.

"Won't talk to me ever, now?" She asked.

"I've never said that." I retorted.

"Then why are you ignoring me?" She questioned.

"It's not what you think, how can I ignore you?"

"Yes it's exactly what I think.. You are avoiding me. I can understand your feelings, but you should also try to understand mine. The way you always looked at me, the way you cared for me, the way you followed me, nothing was hidden from me and the truth is that I liked it too. I kept waiting for your proposal but it never came. If you had asked me before I even met Pratap I would've given you a serious thought but when I saw him, I lost myself. In the first glance itself, I lost my heart him. He had all the qualities that I always dreamt of in my Mr. Perfect. He is stylish, smart and cute too!" She talked obsessively.

He is smart and cute, but what about me? I thought but said nothing.

She continued to narrate her story, "When I first saw him, I jsut wanted to go talk to him immediately. I wanted to see him all the time. Something inside me was telling me that he was the boy of my dreams. When I noticed that his eyes were often on my too, I felt nervously excited. I had never felt that way before."

She kept going.

"Then one day he came to me and said, '*Hey Riya! What's up?*'.

'*Riya? Who is Riya?*' I had questioned him surprised. '*You are not Riya? But you look exactly like her.*' I knew he was lying just to get a chance to talk to me and I appreciated it because I wanted to talk to him too.

'*Really?*' I had smiled.

'*Yes. Believe me. But you look more beautiful than her. Your eyes and lips are prettier than hers.*' He started to flirt with then."

She was cheerfully telling her story but was unaware of my inner turmoil. I was burning from inside.

She continued to narrate. "I only smiled in reply. There was something in me that loved the way that he was flirting with me.

'*If you are not Riya? What is your name?*' he had asked.

"Shipra", I told him. We started talking this way and the same evening, we exchanged our numbers. The graph of our interaction only grew upwards from there.

That day Pratap asked me for a movie, I couldn't resist myself. It was just the two of us that day. I had lied to you about other girls being there with us."

Her words felt like poisonous arrows with which she pierced my heart again and again.

"After Intermediate, I plan to go to Delhi for graduation. On the day of our final match, Pratap came to cheer for me with his father. I met him too."

She was ready to say more but I couldn't take it any longer. I wanted to cry but couldn't bear to be vulnerable in-front of a girl who felt nothing for me.

I resisted the tears and spoke for the first time in that conversation, "It's okay, I am going now."

"Manav, don't be upset. You are my best friend and you always will be." She said softly.

I hate this word, 'friend'. Why do girls always hide behind this word? Why do they always want to befriend the guy who loves them? What do they want from that friendship? Do they want these boys to wander around them and add to their list of fans? Was I one such guy?

I walked away feeling like a gambler who'd lost everything in a gamble. I loved her more than anything in this world, yet what did I get? I had lost her forever. I was living with the hope that she would be mine one day. That hope was also lost that day. I had borne a lot of pain before, but this pain felt unbearable.

When the heart breaks, it doesn't bleed but it hurts more than any other wound or fracture.

With these thoughts, I entered the class. Some of my tears revolted and came down to kiss my cheek. Since it was the lunch break, no one was in the class except for Naina. All the boys must be in the gardens trying to chat up the commerce girls, I thought. She noticed my tears. I wiped them hurriedly and moved to my seat. I had failed to escape her notice, however.

"Manav, come here." She said just what I had feared.

"Yes, what are you doing here alone?" I tried to pull a smile on.

"What has happened?" She asked.

"Nothing. KUCH HONA CHAHIYE THA KYA?" I tried to blow off her question.

"Tell me the real deal. Don't try to hoodwink me with that fake smile." She insisted.

"It is nothing serious." I really didn't want to tell her.

"You are not a good actor at all and you can't hide

your sadness from me. Your innocent eyes are like a mirror in which I can read you clearly. They never lie." She knew me very well.

My eyes became moist again. Does Shipra not see these eyes brimming with love for her. I told Naina everything. All the things about Shipra and me. What my feelings were for her and how Pratap had come and destroyed my world. "Tell me Naina, where was I lacking? Why couldn't she respect my feelings?"

Before Naina could say anything in consolation, the bell rang and students started to fill in the classroom. I stood and rushed towards my place. "Talk to you later." I told her.

That whole day, Naina couldn't get chance to talk to me but I could feel her gaze on me. Whenever our eyes met, she averted her gaze gently.

That evening, I saw Shipra at the coaching centre. She looked stunning in a pink top and blue jeans, but my eyes could not see the same way anymore. It was the first time that I saw her and felt no flutter in my heart. I averted my eyes from her quickly. For the first time, I didn't sit parallel to her. I went to sit on the last bench. She noticed this and turned back to look at me wordlessly. She might have understood that she had lost her right to talk to me. Ankit and Sagar sat on either side of me.

When we walked out after the class, I saw Shipra discussing some-thing with Shristy. I signalled at Ankit to leave. The three of us sat on the bike and left. For the first time we did not follow her to her house and had left the coaching class before her.

Everything had changed. I had changed. She had changed. Situations had changed. Things between us had changed. The love for her in my heart had changed. Her heart had changed too. Nothing was like it used to be before.

School, coaching, home, everything felt like it was coming to bite me each day. I wanted to run away from everything. I wanted to run away from myself. I was lonely.

Hospital again

* * *

I was shaken awake from my thoughts by the ward boy who told me that Shipra had been shifted to ward number 32-A.

"How is she?" I asked eagerly.

"Go and ask the nurse. A doctor is waiting for me." He left.

I entered ward 32-A. A doctor was standing near the bed with some sheets of paper in her hand. Shipra lay unconscious on the bed. How beautiful she was! I couldn't take my eyes away from her cute face. Her head was covered in bandages. My eyes grew point thinking that I was responsible for her piteous condition. I stepped closer and stroke her face gently.

"Bring these medicines and give them to nurse." The Doctor handed me the prescription.

I couldn't read, for the life of me, what she wrote on it.

"When will she come to her senses?" I asked the Doctor.

"Don't worry, she is all right and will regain consciousness in the next two-three hours." She replied kindly.

I returned with the medicines and handed them over to the nurse. She took down the glucose bottle and injected some medicine in it. I observed her closely. She then took a needle and roughly penetrated it in the vein in Shipra's wrist.

"Easy" I cried out as if she has stuck the needle in me. She gave me a stern look that said, "Don't try to teach me, I do this daily".

I sat on a stool near Shipra's bed. I gazed at her beautiful face Randall those feelings from years ago came rushing back. No one could be a beautiful as she was! I lost myself in memories once again.

Chapter– 6
Why can't you understand me like she does?

* * *

The broken heart made me grow terribly lonely. The same heart that throbbed with excitement every morning, now made me lean against the railing of the corridor and stare melancholically at the grass and flowers below. Wind-swept and happy, they seemed to dance and laugh at my piteous condition. They seemed to say, "Look at us. Lovers pluck us to gift us to their beloved and we sacrifice ourselves to fulfil their desire, then why can't you be like us too? Why can't you be happy for Shipra and Pratap? You should stay away from them."

A girl's voice broke my chain of thought.

"Hey! Manav."

I turned around to see Naina, standing right behind me with a cute smile on her face. Her smile was like a drop of water on the burning desert of my heart. One part of my mind told me that she was very beautiful but another contradicted that she is nothing compared to Shipra. Who could dare compete with Shipra's smile? *If your lost your heart to an ass, even angels can't entice you.*

"Hey! Where are you lost?" She asked waving her hand in front of my face.

"Nowhere," I replied dully.

"Really? I have been standing here for the last 5 minutes but you didn't notice me."

"Sorry, I was looking at flowers."

"Can't you stop thinking about her?" She asked seriously looking straight into my eyes.

"I am not thinking about her." I lied.

"Yesterday you asked me where you lacked?" She picked up the conversation from where we had left it the previous day. I was not looking forward to it. "Actually, your love lacks nothing. Only a lucky girl would deserve such love but she was foolish enough to let it go. She didn't deserve your love."

"She is lucky to have Pratap's love."

"I can assure you that no one can love her more than you." She assured me.

"Seriously? Why makes you think so?" I asked joyfully.

"Because I have seen how much you cared for her. You never let her out of your sight. I can still see it in your eyes." She looked into my eyes.

This took me by surprise. We had only talked a couple of times before. How could she have known so deeply about me?

Why couldn't Shipra see this love in my eyes for her? Before I could say anything, the bell interrupted again and we rushed for our morning assembly.

I caught Naina looking towards me several times during the class. Whenever our eyes met, she remove her gaze hurriedly. *Why was she looking at me? She knew I loved*

Shipra, then why? No, perhaps she is only looking to make sure that I am okay.

At lunch, I caught myself staring at the flowers again. There was something about them, some unique attraction that they held for me that I couldn't disengage myself from them. Naina came and stood beside me.

"What are you gazing at?" She asked.

"Nothing, look at those flowers. They know that they are going to wilt in the evening yet they bloom brightly now, as if smiling at the world." I said, my eyes cast down.

"They teach us that all of us will leave the world one day but while we are here, alive and breathing, we should spread our fragrance in the form of good deeds and live out our days happily." She explained like a literature professor.

"Wow! You are a proper philosopher now." I laughed.

She smiled in response. "Have you finished your lunch?" She asked.

"No, I don't have an appetite." I said.

"That is not good. You have to eat your lunch." She insisted.

"Really, I am not hungry."

"You are starving yourself for a girl who doesn't even care about you." She said accusatively.

"That is not it. Is it necessary to drag her name in everything?" I said, irritated.

"Sorry, Don't shout. I am not interested in uttering her name each time but you have to eat", she said forcefully.

"Please, Naina. Try…" Before I could complete my sentence she interrupted me.

"Swear on me and our friendship. You have to eat."

Why do these stupid girls try to lock us in with swears. Why don't they understand that swears are useless? If they were true, God would be the first to die.

I didn't want to hurt her feelings so followed her quietly to the class, took out my lunch box and started to eat. She sat next to me and looked at me eating.

"Aaaa..", she opened her mouth. "One bite please", she requested.

I smiled at her innocent attempt to cheer me up. I took a piece of bread with some veggies and fed her.

"Very tasty, your mother is a wizard cook," she said still chewing. I smiled, "Do you want more? Open your mouth."

"No, now it's my turn to feed you. Open your mouth", she said, smiling.

She looked very cute and innocent sitting so close next to me that I could smell the fragrance of her body. If Shipra had not occupied my heart so intensely, I would have fallen for Naina.

I opened my mouth but before she could feed the morsel to me, Shipra entered in the class and froze at the door. She looked at us for a second, catching us in that moment of intimacy, and then felt uttering a simple "Oops".

My heart ached to see her turning away like that. What would she think about me now? Wouldn't she believe that I was after Naina now? She must think of me a casual flirtatious type who started following Naina after I got rejected by herself. I swallowed the bite that Naina had put in my mouth with great difficulty. I didn't want to sit with Naina anymore. I did not have problem with her but I did not want anyone else to think shit about us. I finished my lunch quickly and rushed outside the class to wash my hands. Naina went to sit at her place.

We had physical education right after lunch. When Mishra Sir entered the room, the whole class sang in unison ,"Games, Sir".

"Quiet", Mishra sir smiled, "Let's do some theory

today, else you won't have anything to write in the exam."

"No sir, games!" we shouted again.

"Okay, come but no one will shout", he agreed.

Everyone rushed towards the ground happily.

Boys ran towards the sports room to get things to play with. Only a few girls went towards the sports room, the others sat on the stairs in groups and started talking.

I dragged myself towards the ground. There was a time when I was the first to run to the volleyball field but now I was frightened of it. I wanted to put as much distance a possible between the volleyball court and myself because it reminded me of Shipra. It seemed threatening. It reminded me of the first time I ever had her practice with me, how I made her attempt the ball, how we trained together. These memories seemed to scathe me from inside and burn away my happiness.

The same fire blazed at my heart when I saw Shipra coming towards the field with a volley-ball in her hand. I shifted my gaze towards the cricket pitch where some of my classmates were playing. Rajiv, Rajesh and Rahul were as passionate about cricket as I was about volleyball.

I was admiring Rajiv's batting when Naina came and sat beside me.

"You are here. Don't you want to play?" I asked, turning towards her.

"Have you ever even seen me playing?" she asked.

"No. Why is that?" I asked again.

"Not interested." She said nonchalantly.

I smiled in response.

"What about you? Never before have I seen you off the Volleyball court, even when you have been sick.". My madness for volleyball hadn't escaped her attention.

"I am not going to play this sport anymore." I muffled sadly.

"Why?"

"I don't like it now."

"ISHQ ruined me 'GHALIB', I wasn't half bad a player myself." She reformed one of Mirza Ghalib's couplets in my favour.

It made me chuckle. "It's not like that, yaar."

"Forget that, but tell me one thing", she sat close to me.

"Yes?" I looked at her. Those big attractive and animated eyes captured my attention.

"Why can't you move on? You know she will never return to your life again. There are so many other girls. Forget her and consider someone else." She was right but her words felt like pointy arrows sticking at my heart.

"I can't control who I fall in love with. Love is like blind worship." I paused. "One more thing, I don't think I will ever forget her."

"Why? When you indulge with another girl, she will automatically be out of your mind."

"She is not just in my mind, she is in my soul. I feel her presence in every vein running in my body, every drop of blood. I inhale and ex-hale her with every breath I take." I almost yelled, my heartbeat picking up pace.

"How can anyone love someone so deeply?" She muffled under her breath.

I ignored her words and continued obsessively, "I have told her that I love her. I love her more than I can express with words. My soul won't allow me to repeat these words to someone else. I have already resigned my heart and myself to her." I couldn't understand what triggered this outburst.

She was staring at me as if I had horns on my head.

"Sorry, I said too much."

"May God bless me with a lover like you." She

sighed.

"Like me? You will get someone better than me." I said.

"No one can be better than you because no one can love a girl more than you do." She said assuredly.

"That's probably not true at all but everyone should fall in love once. Love can be wonderful." I said.

"Shipra betrayed you. She broke your heart. You gave up playing your favourite sport because of her. You are in this condition because of love. And yet you say that love can be wonderful. What kind of a person are you?!" She looked at me surprised.

"Just because you can't reach the grapevine, you cannot dismiss the grapes as sour!

My love hasn't vanished from my heart. I still love to remember her." I explained.

Before Naina could react to my madness, the bell rang and we rushed back towards our class. Each time I saw Shipra, I felt like a fish out of water, my breath knocked out of me, gasping for air. She was walking a little way ahead of me, volleyball in hand. I turned to look at Naina and me together. I removed my gaze from her quickly. I didn't have the courage to face those eyes again. Since she had accepted Pratap, we had only talked once. Shipra had tried to talk to me a couple of times but I tried my best to avoid her. I felt that if I started talking to her again, my feelings for her will resurface and I would end up hurting myself again.

When I entered the class, I saw a group of girls, including Naina and Shipra, crowded around a desk on which there was a spinning water bottle. I was surprised to see both fire and water involved to ardently over a game of Truth and Dare. I went to stand near the lecture desk. The tip of the bottle was pointed towards Jaya. Shipra dared her to kiss the floor twice. The whole class roared with laughter when she sat down to kiss the floor. I too couldn't resist a chuckle too.

The bottle was spun again and it rested pointing towards Shipra this time. As Shipra opted for dare, Jaya shouted, "I will ask, I will ask."

"Hold Manav's hand and propose to him." It was her revenge. She must have known about us and deliberately pushed Shipra into an uncomfortable situation.

"Don't drag me into this", I refused to be the part of their game.

"No, no. She has to propose to you." The girls shouted in unison. Naina was one amongst them too.

"Fine! I will do it." Shipra accepted.

My heart skipped a beat and then started racing. She walked towards me. I couldn't remove my eyes from her face and stared like a fool. She stopped right in front of me. I hadn't been this close to her in a long time. She looking m straight in the eyes for a few seconds before extending her hand towards me. I gave my hand submissively into hers, hypnotized.

"Manav. I love you." She said and cast down her eyes.

She was probably not saying these words for the first time. Pratap must have heard these words quite enough by now, but it was a first for me. The one girl whom I have loved most truly, the one from whom I had waited to hear those magical words from, she finally said those words. I had waited for this for the longest time. I felt as if time had stopped and the air blew gently with a unique fragrance around me. I felt lost in the depth of her eyes. I returned to my senses when she tried to withdraw her hand. My whole world seemed to go snatching away with that withdrawal. I did not have a choice but to let it go. The perfect world of my imagination had no place in reality. I left her hand and she walked back to her place.

Their game resumed. I silently thanked that bottle, the game and Jaya for her challenge, that ended up giving me a memory. Shipra too had, unknowingly, granted me a memory with which I could spend the rest of my life. The way she held my hand, the way she looked into my eyes the way her lips trembled a little before she uttered those magical words and the way she blushed and cast down her eyes; these little moments of intimacy were sufficient for me. I continued to look at her, lost. She was laughing, jumping and enjoying the game unaware of the storm that she had triggered in me.

Diwali was just a week away. All the shops set up a display of fire crackers and the houses were bedecked in fairy lights. Our school was not immune to the spirit of the festival either. Despite close inspections and multiple warnings, a cracker or two went off each day within the premise. Students had cleverly planted these crackers in the lavatories, delaying the ignition time, so that they had ample window to flee the scene before it went off. The teachers had a hard time picking out the culprits.

The Principal was specially annoyed with these instances. One day, during the morning assembly he brought up the topic to discuss in front of the whole school. He said, "This type of nuisance will not be tolerated. Those who are caught involved in the bursting of crackers will be expelled from this institution. There will be no grace given. I am warning you." Before he could complete his speec, a cracker burst in the toilet on the upper deck. The whole assembly burst out laughing. All the teachers ran to-wards the spot but this time too, there was nobody to be found. Principal Sir left the stage in anger.

When we turned to go to class, Naina yelled from behind, "Manav, stop."

I turned, "Yes?"

"I have something to talk to you about." She tugged at my wrist and almost dragged me aside.

"What is it? Why have you dragged me here?" I asked loudly.

"Sssh", she kept a finger on her lips. "Be quiet. I also want a cracker."

"What? But why?" I asked in surprise.

"I will plant one in the girls' washroom." She smiled.

"Have you gone mad?"

"What? It will be fun. No cracker has ever been burst in the girls' washroom yet." She looked excited.

The idea interested me. Nothing will surprise the teachers more than finding such mischief in the girls' washroom. I smiled at the wicked thought.

"Okay, I will bring you one tomorrow." I accepted happily.

The next day, I brought a cracker and a piece of mosquito coil, to light it with, in my bag. We stood outside waiting for the morn-ing assembly bell to ring but the routine was interrupted by an untimely announcement. "Everybody is instructed to return to their classes. The morning assembly will be held after one hour." This has never happened before; the classes never started before the morning assembly. Our class teacher signalled at us to come inside the class.

He entered the classroom and rumbled sarcastically, "AAJ KAL K BACHE SAB ATANK-WADI HO GYE HAIN. BOMB FOD RAHE HAIN. (Students these days have taken to terrorism, bursting crackers (bombs) in campus). Some excellent fool-proof arrangements they have." We laughed, unsuspecting. He smiled too.

"On the Principal's orders, we are going to check your bags this morning. Let's see who comes from a terrorist back-ground". He smiled menacingly.

Everyone laughed but my heart sank. The cracker in my bag felt like a glowing piece of hot coal. I was frightened and thought that there was no hope for survival anymore. No one could save me now. I started praying to the Almighty under my breath to save me, just this once.

Pandey sir called for our head boy and head girl with their bags. We were lucky to have them both in our section. Prakharanshu, a studious bespectacled kid, was our head boy, He was always punctual, silent, dedicated and attentive in the class. He was a talented but boring person. Sonika, our head girl, was his polar opposite. Her round face and fair complexion made her look like an angel. She had lovely eyes, thin red lips, stylish hair and her face always had a smile on it. She was beautiful and interesting. One could never get bored talking to her.

Both of them went to Pandey sir with their bags. They had nothing but stationary items. He instructed them to check our bags. "Prakharanshu will check the girls' bags and Sonika will check the boys' bags."

Sonika started with Manjeet, who was sitting on the first bench. My heart sped as she drew closer. I could see myself standing outside the school with a suspension letter in hand.

She arrived at my desk and opened the first chain of my bag. It had nothing but pens and pencils. She opened the second chain and her eyes went straight to the green cracker tied to the mosquito coil. She looked at me questioningly. I looked at her with pleading eyes and a miserable expression. I shook my head in dread. I felt like a cattle preparing for slaughter, left at the mercy of the butcher.

She went straight for the cracker and my heart revolted, "BITCH EK BAAR CHOR DETI TO KYA HO JATA?" I thought. She withdrew her hand and sneaked the cracker into her pocket. I wanted to kiss her hands.

When Pandey sir left the class, I went to Sonika and sat on my knees. One might have thought that I was going to propose but I just cried out 'Thank you, Thank you' several times.

She tugged at my shirt and pulled me up. "So you are the guy who was bursting crackers in school?"

"No, No", I protested.

"So?"

"Naina asked me to bring one for her because she wanted to plant one in the girls' washroom."

She looked towards Naina, who was sitting between Ruchi and Nayla.

"Yes, let's do it. BAHUT MZA AAYAGA" She said excitedly.

"No, if someone finds out, there will be a huge problem." Sonika refused.

"How will anyone find out if we don't tell?" Ruchi supported Naina.

"Yes, it will be great fun." Abhinav, Prakharanshu's benchmate, also supported the girls.

Slowly the whole class was buzzing excitedly with this conspiracy. Every one promised that they would never mention this to anyone else.

"What if Sir asks?" Prakharanshu tried to object but I intervened.

"Guardian, please not this time. The whole class is ready. Don't butt your leg in."

"Yes guardian, please keep quiet." The whole class shouted.

"Fine! I won't. Do whatever you want." He resigned.

"Ruchi, let's plant this in the washroom right now." Naina took the tiny green ball from Sonika and pulled

Ruchi away with her.

"I will also come." Nayla yelled from behind.

They went out of the class. At the same time, the warning bell rang and we left for the assembly field.

The teachers had managed to confiscate some crackers from other classrooms. They had also found other objectionable items like tobacco, cigarettes and mobile phones from some bags. The guilty students were made to stand aside during the assembly. I would have accompanied them too, if Sonika hadn't been kind to me. I thanked her again from the depth of my heart.

After the morning routine, Principal Sir came to the stage and said, "We were worried about the cracker situation so we decided to check your bags but the thing we got from your bags makes us even more worried. If you are smoking and taking drugs at this age, how will your future turn out? Look at these people who will become old before their age, as they've started smoking and taking drugs." He indicated towards the row of boys who were standing separately. "I am not going to allow these bastards in my school anymore. I will call their parents and will hand over the things we found in their bags to them. After all, they should be aware of what their sons are upto." He said with heavy sarcasm.

We returned to our classes soon after his threatening speech.

"Have you planted it?" I asked Ruchi as she entered the class.

"Yes."

"When will it burst?"

"How can I tell? We have ignited the coil. Let's wait and watch." She said.

Just then,our bio teacher A.K Pandey, entered the class and enquired of us, "What is going on?"

"Nothing sir," We separated and rushed to our places.

"BOMB BANANA TO NAHI SIKH RAHA NA?" He asked Ruchi with a smile.

"Yes, sir!" The whole class bellowed in affirmation.

"This is a bad thing and you should not get involved in such stupidity. You come here to study, you should focus on that. Get a good job after you finish your education. AB TO BACHE PAISA CHAAPNE KE MACHINE HO GYE HAIN. Aspire for the best."

We laughed. We loved his amusing statements and waited excitedly for them.

Before he could say another word, we heard a loud boom from down the corridor. He put his hand on his head and said, "LO EK OR FATA." He rushed out of the class to join the other teachers.

All of us exchanged secret knowing glances. We were not scared, we knew out secret was safe. We had done it. This collective unity made me feel proud.

The next day, the teachers checked our bags again but found nothing. Nobody dared to sneak anything in after the threat of the previous day. No more crackers were heard bursting in the school.

"Manav, I am going to join Pandey sir's coaching class from today." Naina chirped like a sweet little bird.

"Why? You are already so good at mathematics." I blurted.

"So? Do you have a problem? You only want Shipra to be there?" She said with fake anger.

"Are you crazy? What problem could I have if you decide to attend that class? In fact, it will make me very happy. Please come to Pandey sir's coaching madam, I welcome you in advance." I bowed in front of her.

I was suddenly struck by a thought. *Why had*

she decided to go to Pandey sir's class? Why was she taking interest in me? I had noticed that she was always on the look out to talk to me. *Had she some feelings for me?*

Was I over-thinking it? She knew everything. She knew how much I loved Shipra. How could she still pursue me?

That evening, I saw Naina arriving on her white scooty to Pandey Sir's class. She had kept her word. Her wind-swept hair and fancy black sunglasses made her look very pretty. She caught everyone's eye immediately. I smiled proudly when she stopped her scooty in front of me and cooed "Hey!"

"You look amazing. 'EKDAM MAST' ", I said smiling.

"Really?" She took off her sunglasses and looked at me with her big eyes. She had applied Kajal this evening that only accentuated her beauty more. I had never seen such genuinely beautiful eyes before. If Shipra had not been in my heart, I would have sunk in her big eyes.

"Where are you lost?" She asked and pulled me out of my reverie.

"Nowhere, Naina your eyes are very beautiful especially with kohl in them." I couldn't hide what my heart said.

"Are you flirting with me?" She raised an eyebrow.

"No madam. How can I ever dare to?" I pretended fright.

"Better be careful." She said with a princess-attitude. She was only short of a province to be a real princess.

"Let's not get late for class." I signalled at her to follow me.

She parked her scooty and came walking towards me. I was seeing her out of the school uniform for the first time.

She looked completely different. Her bosom looked ample in her red top and her tight white jeans attracted everyone's eyes. I couldn't resist either.

We entered the coaching and Naina went to sit on the first bench as it was vacant. When she saw me looking for a seat behind, she gave me a questioning look. She pointed towards an empty seat on the first bench in the boys' row. I joined my hand and bowed to her. I wasn't going to sit on the first bench and listen to Pandey sir's boring lectures.

If one sits on the first bench, the teachers think that he or she is the most sincere and intelligent student. Their eyes are always on them and they are the prime target for all their questions. One also has to nod in assurance every time they ask whether the topic they just covered was well understood.

I sat on the last bench with Ankit and Sagar. Naina turned back to look at me. I smiled as our eyes met. Shipra sat just behind Naina. She was very quiet that day. She never turned back to look at me. Perhaps, she was not too pleased with our new batch mate.

After the class, I found Naina standing next to her snooty, waiting. I turned to approach her.

"Oye! Where?" Ankit hollered.

"Just a minute." I said and kept walking towards her. "SALA HARAMI!" I heard him murmur.

"Hey! Is everything fine? Did you like your first day here?" I asked.

"Yes, everything was good but tell me one thing, why didn't you sit on the first bench?" She hadn't moved on from that.

"I love the back bench. It is lucky for me." I replied with smile.

"So funny." She distorted her face in a grimace.

"I have to go now," I said and indicated towards

Ankit and Sagar.

"They are waiting for me."

"Come with me, I will drop you." She smiled.

"Seriously? How did I get so lucky to sit with you on your scooty?" I said dramatically.

"Don't be smart. I am serious. Please come, no?" She request-ed.

"Okay, since you insist, I will come with you." I agreed.

"Yes, my Lord please. My clan will be obliged if you sit on my scooty." She retorted in a dramatic manner.

"Let me just ask Ankit and Sagar."

"Why? Do you do everything with their permission?" She asked snidely.

I didn't like her tone but gently replied, "It's not like that, but they are my friends. I always go with them. If I do not go today, I owe them an explanation."

"It's okay, don't get so serious now."

Why do girls ask so many questions when the answers are of no consequence to them?

I turned towards Ankit and Sagar and saw Shipra standing at some distance with her friends. I knew she had her eyes on Naina and me. When she turned to look at me this time, our eyes met and she quickly averted her gaze.

"I am going with Naina." I told Ankit and Sagar.

"Really? Where?"Ankit asked.

"She said that she will drop me" I replied.

"Oh! Now SHE will drop you? Don't need friends anymore, do you? "

"HARAMI, I don't mean that. She insisted, so…" I left the sentence hanging.

"Yes, yes you are right. Go with her but make sure you sit close to her", Sagar came close to me and spoke in a sexual tone "And hold her waist tight."

"HAT SALA THARKI," I pushed him away.

"Seriously I have had this dream to sit with Shalu like that but you're more lucky. What can I do? Go man, enjoy." He pretended to be sad. The three of us laughed.

"See you tomorrow" I smacked Sagar on his head.

They sat on the bike and rode off. I rushed towards Naina. At the same time, Shalu accelerated her scooty too and left with Shipra.

"Let's go" I said looking at Naina.

She threw the key of her scooty towards me giving me the front seat. I threw the keys back at her, "I don't know how to ride."

"What?" She said surprised. "You don't know how to ride yet?"

"NAAH" I replied carelessly.

"Oh God!" She stroked her hair with her hand. She turned on the ignition and I sat behind her.

"You are old enough and you don't know how to ride yet? How shameful!" She teased.

"I don't think there is any shame in not being able to ride." "You are stupid." She said, irritated. "Yes I am." I said.

"Do you want to learn? I can teach you. " She said. I don't know why she was so insistent.

"No" I refused straight away.

"Why?"

"I will fall and get hurt." I said innocently.

She started laughing loudly.

"What's so funny?" I asked.

"Nothing" She curbed her laughter. "Are you mad? Why will you fall?" She asked gently.

"I don't know, I just have a feeling. Due to this fear I never bothered to learn in the first place." I said.

"Don't be afraid. I will sit behind you, you won't

fall." She kept asserting.

"Anyone who has a friend like Naina can never fall." I smiled.

"Stop buttering me up." She halted her scooty.

"What happened? Why have we stopped?" I asked gingerly.

"Come to the driving seat. Try once." She insisted.

"No, leave it. Please." The fear of falling was still strong in my veins.

"No, come here. You have to drive." She commanded.

"I will, I promise, but not today. From tomorrow, I will learn." I said resigned.

She laughed. "You are scared like a little kid. I will not listen to any of your excuses tomorrow."

She insisted on dropping me to my house but I knew my society was not so liberal and open-minded to take the matter of a girl driving a boy around, lightly.

I asked her to drop me a little way away from my house.

The next day, after coaching, she was giving me a ride home again when Shipra and Shalu crossed us on their scooty. Naina sat upright, adjusted the rear-view mirror, gripped the handle tightly and accelerated. The scooty shot forward like a bullet. We crossed them in a few seconds. Naina had her eyes on the rear view-mirror and saw Shalu approaching swiftly from behind.

"Oho, race! That too with me?" She murmured and sped-her scooty.

"Naina. What are you doing?" I shouted in her ear.

"You just watch. They will never be able to cross us." She turned her head to scream at me.

"Naina leave it. Let them go." I yelled from behind.

"Why?"

"Because I am telling you to." I kept my hand on her shoulder.

"Manav!" She shouted irritated.

"Naina.." I exclaimed with affection. Just then Shalu's Scotty crossed us.

"They have won just because of you." She sulked.

"Forget it." I said. Just then she turned left from the 'REDMA CHOWK'.

"Oye! Where?" I shouted.

"Chianki aerodrome." She replied softly.

"Why?" I asked.

"You are going to learn how to ride a scooty today." She replied.

"No, No. Who approved of that?" I could feel the terror rising in me.

"What? Yesterday you gave me your word." She stopped her scooty.

"Is it necessary?" I asked.

"Yes, why are you so scared? I will be behind you." She insisted.

"Okay, but not the aerodrome." I refused to go there.

"Why?" She asked.

"There would be bikers there who might pass vulgar comments."

"Then where?"

"Let's go to the housing colony ground." I suggested.

"No, it is too near to my house." Naina's place was about five hundred meters from the said ground.

"No one will see. Your father is not sitting at the ground as a vigilante."

"It's not about my father. But if anyone else sees and recognises me, they will inform him of it." She tried to explain.

"Don't be so tense. No one will see." I said stubbornly.

"Okay, let's go. JO HOGA, DEKHA JAYGA." She accelerated towards the housing colony ground.

Teenagers take the worse decisions with this attitude.

We stopped in the middle of the ground. She handed over the scooty to me. I sat on the driving seat with trembling hands and feet. She sat behind me.

"This is the break and that is the accelerator on the right." She indicated towards my hands form behind.

"I know all this." I retorted.

"Good. Then accelerate slowly" she leaned over my back to put both her hands on mine over the the handle. I could feel her chest pressing into my back.

"Accelerate, now." She rotated the accelerator from over my hand. The scooty crawled forward. I felt a strange pleasure in the whole activity. My hands under hers, her body leaning over mine. As I gained balance, she withdrew her hands. The fear of falling had gone away. I rode around the edges of the ground. A little boy appeared in front of us so she placed her hands on mine again and pulled at the break. We rode like like for about a half hour and during this period she leaned on my back several times.

I handed the scooty back to her and sat behind. She accelerated.

"Driving is not that difficult." I screamed in the wind.

"I told you, but you were crying like a child. *I will fall.*" She teased me and laughed.

"It's not funny. Every human being has some kind of phobia."

"I don't have any phobia."

"You did not hear me properly. I said 'Human being.'" I laughed.

"Very funny." she distorted her face.

Just then she turned towards 'BAIRIYA CHOWK'.

"Oye! Where?" I asked. "We have to go the opposite way."

"I know, but we are going to HANUMAN MANDIR first."

"Temple? Why?" I asked again.

"Stupid. Why does one go to the temple?"

"But why at this time and that too after having eaten?" I had the belief that one could only go to the temple after taking a bath and with an empty stomach.

"Who told you that you can't go to temple after having eaten?" She adjusted the rear view mirror to see my face.

"Everyone" I replied.

"Not everyone, only our saints and pundits. Our religion is sim-ple and straight forward but these priests make it complex for their own benefit."

"Really?" I smiled. I didn't take her words seriously.

"Seriously, they frightening us in the name of religion and God, to extract money from us. It is not their fault alone, all of us agree with their non-sense. They are insensitive men who make business out of a person's death too. They have made up so many rituals in the name of giving peace to the departed soul. They take heavy words like 'SANKALP' and 'DAKSHINA' to demand money. They demand food, household items and even a cow. They justify it by saying that the soul will cross the 'BAITARNI' holding onto the tail of the cow. I don't understand how that is even possible when the cow it itself tied to the house of the priest." She poured out all the bitterness that she had in her heart for the priests and the pundits.

I listened to her seriously. I found myself agreeing with her. Religion should not be a liability.

She continued. "If an innocent crow sits on your head by mistake, they will declare it a bad omen and demand things again in donation. They have a demand list for every occasion."

She would have gone on with her rant but we reached the temple just then. There was a giant statue of HANUMAN JI inside. He carried the mountain Sanjeevni in one hand and a mace in the other. We bowed our heads with hands joined in devotion.

"What did you wish for?" She asked as we came out of the temple.

"I don't believe in wishing" I said straight forwardly.

"Why?"

"God knows everything. Why should I ask him for something explicitly?" I told her.

"You will always be a duffer. God knows everything but he waits till you wish for it. Lord Krishna knows everything but he didn't come to Draupadi's rescue till she beckoned him." She explained

"How do you know all this?" She was far too religiously inclined for a teenager.

"My mother is religious. She tells me all these stories and has developed this habit in me to go the temple daily." She explained.

"I respect her for having invested in you this way."

"Really? Do you want to meet her?" She asked smiling.

"No. No. Do you want to see me dead?" I pretended to be afraid.

"Why?"

"I have heard that your mother is very strict and even uses harsh words when she gets angry." I told her what I had heard from Ankit and Sagar.

"Are you stupid? Who told you all this? Meet her

once, she is very sweet." I thought she would snap but she said this very calmly.

"Is she really that nice?" I asked.

"Yes,whenever I get angry and refuse to eat, she drags me to her lap and feeds me with her own hands. I am still a little kid for her. And I get angry only to sit in her lap. I love it when she feeds me with her own hands. I am her only child, that is why she is so protective of me. This is why the Vishal case got out of hand. Which mother will not get angry when somebody attacks their daughter with harsh words?." I could see that she shared a deep relationship with her mother. "My mom is not bad, but these students have spiced up some stupid rumours to make her look like it. My mom is my idol. It is she who has given me the courage to stand up to anyone who misbehaves with me."

"I saw your courage on the first day of school itself, when you shouted at Ankit." I said.

"And you did not even come back to take your bag." She laughed, remembering the incident.

"You were so angry, that I got frightened."

Chatting, we reached 'G.L.A' College, which was at a walking distance from my home so I asked Naina to drop me there.

"Can't I drop you to your house?" She asked.

"I don't want any nonsense gossip to start about us." I said dismissively.

"What a coward you are!" She snided.

"You will feel the same way if I come to your house."

"Never. You can come any time. I will welcome you from my door." She chirped.

"No. No. I can't come. Your dragon mummy will be there." I laughed loudly.

"I will kill you." She reached for my neck.

"Okay, okay, I was only joking yaar."

"She is very nice." She insisted.

"Yes, I know" I smiled and turned towards my house.

"See you tomorrow." I waved at her.

"Okay bye, take care." She waved back.

The next evening, we were at the field again. I rode the scooty and Naina sat behind me. I left the brake and turned up the accelerator. The scooty shot forward like a bullet.

"Slow, slow! Accelerate slowly." Naina shouted.

I left the accelerator on her command. The sooty jerked to a stop and the inertia forced Naina against my back.

"What are you doing?" She said, annoyed.

"I am sorry. What can I do? Sometimes it moves fast and now it has stopped." I said sheepishly.

A wide grin appeared on her face, hearing my innocent re-ply. "See, leave the brake slowly and accelerate at the same time." She leaned over again to hold the accelerator and brake.

After a week when, I had mastered the accelerator and the clutch, Naina asked me to drive on the road. I hesitated first, but then agreed since driving on the same circular path of the field was growing boring each day.

"Be careful, I can hit anyone." I chuckled.

"Don't worry I am with you. Just keep clear of the vehicles." She assured me.

I turned the scooty around and eased it onto the road from the dusty ground. I felt the fright coming back to creep at my heart. Whenever a heave truck or bus came by way, I stopped on the side of the road to let it pass.

"What are you so frightened of? There is enough space.

You should keep driving." She commanded, sitting

behind.

"They come at me in such speed that I feel like they will pass over me, crushing me underneath."

"Nothing will happen. They have eyes and brakes too.

Don't be afraid."

I rode till REDMA CHOWK and returned safely. I easily for next two days too. It boosted my confidence and I thought to myself, "Not everyone needs to fall to learn how to ride."

In my newly gained confidence, I was speeding on the road one day. Naina had already told me to reduce the speed several times but I didn't listen to her. Everything was going fine but then suddenly a bike appeared from the left turn and took me by surprise. I got flustered and nervous and lost control of the scooty.

"Manav!" Naina yelled and turned the handle to the left, hurriedly and applied the brakes at the same time. The vehicle turned more than it should have, the tires screeched and we were thrown off the side of the road. The scooty went sliding ahead with us. All of it happened in a fraction of a second. When I regained my senses, I found the scooty on top of us. I pulled my legs out and straightened the scooty. Naina stood up and winced in pain.

"What happened? Are you okay?" I approached Naina hurriedly.

"My ankle seems to have twisted. It's hurting badly." She held my shoulder to support herself.

She exclaimed suddenly, pointing at my hand, "Your hand is bleeding. You must be in so much pain!"

"I am okay. It's minor. I am worried for you." I supported her weight on my shoulder.

"I am fine," she left my shoulder and stood by herself.

"Naina, what has happened?" a voice pulled us back to reality. A crowd had gathered around us and a man, who must have known Naina, came forward.

"Are you okay?" He came closer and asked again.

"Yes, I am fine." She said and took the scooty in her command. She didn't want to engage with that man any further.

I sat quietly behind her. She noticed my legs when I sat on the scooty.

"Your leg is also bleeding," she said. "We must see a doctor".

"It's nothing. There is no need of doctor." I said.

"Have you gone mad? We are going to the doctor." She was stubborn.

"Naina, please…" before I could complete my sentence she shouted, "Be quiet. We are going."

"Yes, madam" I was a slave to her commands.

"Everything seems to be a joke to you." She complained.

"Drop me at the clinic on the way to my house I will manage from there."

She agreed, after a long argument. She wanted to accompany me all the way to my house.

"By the way, who was that man there who knew your name?" I asked her.

"My neighbor."

"What if he tells your mother about the accident?" I asked con-cerned.

"Don't worry I will tell her everything myself before he can." She smiled.

"Then your dragon mom…" I started but she interrupted me, "She is nice."

"Sorry. I know." I smiled.

She smiled back.

The next day we were waiting outside the coaching, when I saw Naina arrive with a woman sitting on the back seat. Ankit elbowed me, "That's Naina's mom."

My face grew pale. Naina must have told her about yesterday's accident and she must have come here to rebuke me for it. I was frightened of the unavoidable confrontation.

Her entry to our coaching centre was similar to that of Parshurama 'sat Sita's *Swayamvara*, after Rama broke Lord Shiva's bow. The same fear could be seen on the faces of boys here, which once must have housed the faces of princes who had come to marry Sita.

Everyone knew of the terror that she carried with her persona. *Who was she going to objurgate or slap today?* Everyone tried to hide themselves.

Naina parked the scooty and her mother looked around, as if searching for the boy who injured her loving daughter. That day I figured where Naina got her good looks from. Nobody could have said that this woman was the mother of a mid-teenaged girl. She was extremely beautiful. She must have been more beautiful than Naina in her days. She looked amazingly graceful in her blue 'salwar kameez'.

My anxiety peaked when she came to stand right in front of me.

'NAMASTE, AUNTY.' I blurted out nervously.

"Were you with Naina yesterday?" The calm in her voice was unexpected.

"Yes, aunty" I stammered. "I lost control because of the speed so…." I left the sentence incomplete.

"It's okay beta. Don't worry. It happens sometime but you should be careful." I looked at her, gaping. I expected her to be furious, but she called me 'beta' and quietly made me understand why I shouldn't speed on the road. I didn't say anything. I was looked at her with sheer disbelief.

She continued, "It was good luck that the accident

was minor. If something serious had happened to you or Naina, then? Have you thought about your mother?"

"Sorry aunty." I spoke as I recovered the surprise.

"It's okay. Don't be sorry. I am like your mother too, so I am making you understand. Don't think that I am scolding you." She said with fondness in her voice.

"No aunty. Thankyou." I said without fumbling this time.

Just then a car halted behind me. and interrupted our conversation.

"Okey beta, see you." She put her hand on my head lovingly.

She walked towards the car and called out to Naina before pulling the door shut, "Take care and don't be late."

"Yes mom" Naina waved her hand at her.

My perception of Naina's mother had completely changed.

After coaching, Naina insisted that I ride again. I was still frightening from yesterday's incident but she made it impossibly for me to refuse. I accelerated but did not speed over forty.

"TERI MOM TO BAHUT SUNDAR HAI."(Your mom is very beautiful) I said looking at her face in the rear-view mirror.

"She is my mom, afterall." She chirped with childlike glee on her face.

"She is not at all the monster that my friends had made her out to be. She is very sweet" I told her what I had in my heart.

"Really? Thank you." She said "When mom said that she wanted to meet you, I told her not to scold you, as you are my best friend."

Chatting happily, she dropped me near my home and returned back.

Chapter – 7
In Love Again

* * *

I could comfortably drive the scooty and bike now and it was all because of Naina. From a month, it became our routine to go to the HANUMAN temple and bow our heads, before Naina was to drop me at my place.

Those scooty rides got us a lot closer. We grew a lot more familiar to each other. We were always seen together, shared everything and were very happy in each other's company.

That closeness must have given her the wrong idea.

One day at school, I was standing outside the class as our Hindi teacher had not yet arrived.

"Let's go to the small ground." Naina came and suggested.

"Why?" I asked.

"To bunk the class", she said. I couldn't believe my ears. Naina was a studious girl who I had never thought would think of bunking a class.

Generally, we went to the small ground to bunk classes as it was apart from the main school building and it wasn't very easy to be spotted there. Another alternative was to sit in the bus. For that, you had to have some familiarity with the bus operating staff before-hand. Ankit and I were regular bunkers and were on good terms with Amit Bhaiya, the conductor of bus number four.

Whenever we passed him, we used to ask, "KA BHAIYA, BHABHI KAISI HAI? (Hey brother, how is your wife?)", and more often than not, we got the reply, "JALDI CHA-CHA BANOGE. (You'll be an uncle soon.)"

"Why are we bunking today?" I asked.

"Let's go." She tugged at my wrist. "You are acting as if you are bunking for the first time."

"Yes, indeed. TUM BIGAD RHI HO MUJHE (You are making me indisciplined)." I smiled.

"Very funny. I know you very well. By the way, I have something important to tell you", she said.

We reached the small ground. She went to sit on the cemented stairs under a tree. I plucked some leaves from the tree and dropped them over her head, chanting "OM MANGALAM BHAGWAN VISHNU."

"Manav, please sit. I have something important to say." She said dusting the leaves off her head.

"Tell me." I sat beside her.

"Manav", she looked straight into my eyes. "I have been wanting to tell you this for a long time but couldn't dare to."

"What is it?" I asked

"I like you, Manav."

I was stupefied. Was she going to say the words I always wished to hear from Shipra? "What?" I exclaimed in surprise.

"Yes, Manav." She paused for a few seconds and resumed, "On the first day itself when you introduced yourself and apologised for Ankit's prank, you seemed like a good guy to me. As our friendship strengthened, I started liking the way you talked to me, the way you praised my beauty. It felt like I had someone out there who really looked-out for me, who cared for me and it made me feel special. My started developing feelings for you. Your presence made all the difference in my behaviour, it pleased me; just like it was too dull to be in your absence. Whenever I see you enter the class, my heart chants with happiness."

I was dumb-founded and continued to look at her wordlessly. She continued, "I started dreaming about us, building imaginary castles in the air. But everything crumbled to pieces when Shipra came into your life. The seed that got planted in your heart after that tiff on the stairs, sprouted and grew into a tree in front of my eyes and I was distraught, but helpless. The day you asked me to get her number for you, I can't express how bad I felt! I tried to make you understand but you were blind in her love. I didn't insist further because you were happy.

The day I heard about Shipra and Pratap, I was unable to decide whether I should be happy or sad. I felt bad for you but somewhere deep inside, I was also pleased because I now had the chance to disclose my feelings to you. I have been waiting to tell for a long time how much I love you."

She had poured her heart out to me and it was my turn to speak. I kept quiet for a few seconds. I couldn't decide where to start and what to say. She was my best friend and I didn't want to hurt her. I started softly. "Naina, you are my best friend. I have never looked at you any other way. You already know how much I love Shipra. I have surrendered my heart, soul and everything else to her. I only have one heart which I have given to her. How can I make any promises to you? If I say 'yes', it will be unfair to both Shipra and you." I said all this in one breathe. I didn't understand where these words were coming from, I was generally not so good with them. Perhaps it was my love for Shipra that poured out in front of Naina, when it got the chance.

I continued, "I have her sown deep in my heart. My mind is full of her thoughts and memories. I can't part from them even if I wish for it. Please forgive me, I can't say yes to you. I am sorry."

"This very nature of yours is what has attracted me the most towards you Manav. You love her so much even when you know that she doesn't love you. How can you love her so much? She hurt you yet, you worship her. How can you be so good to her? Boys today easily flirt with two or three girls at a time and you are rejecting me for a girl who doesn't even love you. Please accept my love Manav. Even one percent of the love which you have for Shipra will be enough for me. Please don't discard me and my love like this." She said with pleading eyes.

She sat on her knees and was about to join her hands to beg for her desire but I held both her hands in mine and said, "Please don't do this, else I will never forgive myself." I made her sit on the stairs and sat beside her. I held her left hand. She was quiet and her eyes were cast down, almost on the verge of tears.

"Naina, look here." I held her chin and lifted her face up towards me.

"You say you love me. Now suppose some other guy proposes to you, will you accept his proposal? Will you start loving him and forget all about me?" I asked looking straight into her eyes.

She shook her head, averted her gaze and started digging the earth. I was afraid, I was going to make her cry.

"Then how can I? Naina, you are very good. The boy to whom you commit, will surely be the luckiest boy in the world. But I am not him."

"Don't lie." Tears started rolling down her cheeks

and her voice was choked. “I am as good as her that is why you are refusing me”, she said innocently.

“Don’t talk this way. You are the sweetest.” Before I could say anything else to console her she, clung to me and said, “Manav, I love you. Please don’t abnegate me. I will be all alone without you.” She started weeping and blubbering like a baby.

I didn’t know what to do anymore. I was at a loss of words to console her. I had no choice but to leave her weeping and I did that. I allowed her to vent out her feelings and patted her back gently. How strongly I felt the irony of my situation at that time! I kept pining for someone’s love but did not get it and now someone else was weeping for my love and I was compelled to say No. Naina’s tears was stinging me as harshly as herself. But what could I do? She was begging from a beggar. I had nothing to give her.

Slowly, she controlled herself and sat straight. I wiped away the tears from her cheeks with my hands. My eyes had grown moist too and I wiped them secretly.

“It’ll only make me love you more if you bother yourself with my tears.” She sobbed.

“PAGLI.” I patted fondly on her head.

She rested her head on my shoulder and tucked her hair behind her ear.

When the top of her head touched my cheek, a feeling of love stirred through my heart. When a girl rests her head on a boy’s shoulder, it feels like she has completely surrendered herself, her fate and future to the boy. That’s how I felt. She had exposed her vulnerable side to me. At that time she looked so cute and lovely that my mind counselled me to say Yes to her but immediately my heart intervened, ‘*How could you betray your love for Shipra*’, and I controlled myself.

“Manav, I am not going to leave you.” She murmured

and sat straight.

"What do you mean?" I looked at her.

"I am never going to stop loving you. You don't love me and that's okay. But I will love you till the last breath leaves my body."

"Are you crazy?" I didn't understand whether to shout or to make her understand softly.

She continued as if she hadn't heard me. "Say Yes when you are convinced of the faith in my love. I will wait for you. If my love is sacred and I love you truly, one day you will be mine."

"Don't do this. You will get nothing out of it." I tried to make her understand.

She did not say anything but got up quietly to go to class. The sparkle had gone from her eyes. Her cute, chirpy and mesmerizing face now looked pale and ill. She dragged herself towards the class. I followed her quietly. I knew what she was feeling then. My rejection had hurt her badly.

Love does not hurt you as much as rejection and indifference does.

I decided to keep my distance from Naina and to not talk to her. Being her best friend, I wanted to help her, but couldn't for she could have mistaken it for something else. I wanted her to move on. I wanted her to forget me, to erase her love for me from her heart even though I knew it was impossible.

After coaching that day, I did not go home with her even though I saw her waiting for me. How lonely and helpless she must have felt that day, going home alone.

Next day at school, I tried not to talk to her. She attempted to approach me but I ignored her, pretending I was busy.

After coaching that day she saw me walking away and yelled, "Manav."

I stopped and asked "What?"

"Won't you go with me?" She asked expectantly.

"No, we have some work." I said as I took my place on Ankit's bike. I tapped on his shoulder to accelerate.

"What happened between the two of you? Why have you stopped going home with her?" Ankit asked, turning towards Redma chowk.

"Nothing, She has gone mad." I said dismissively.

"Really?" Sagar leaned forward to look at my face. "At least tell us what happened."

I narrated the whole story with details of what had happened between us.

"What is the problem then? Say Yes to her." Ankit said taking her side.

"Have you seen her? How cute is she!" Sagar also supported him.

"Sexy too." Ankit sighed.

"KAMINA, concentrate on the road." I said annoyed.

"HAYE CHAWANNI!" Sagar laughed. Ankit joined him.

"It all started with this word 'CHAWANNI.'' I said.

"You have to give me a treat. It is my teasing that helped you two come close." Ankit turned back to smile at me.

"LAAT KHAYEGA?" I asked.

Naina had made me the centre of her world. My indifference was killing her from inside. Without knowing this fact, I continued to ignore her. During the lunch break, she came and she tugged at my wrist.

"Have I committed sin by disclosing my feelings to you?" There was a sorrowful seriousness in her tone.

"No, did I ever say that to you?"

"What do you want to prove by not talking to me?"

She asked.

"Who said I am not talking to you? I am talking to you right now." I smiled.

"This does not fool me. You are not talking to me. I am forcing you to do so," she said painfully.

"Look Naina, I think you should forget me and move on." I told her straight-away.

"I can't forget you Manav. Why don't you understand? I love you." She held my hand.

"It's not love, damn it. It's only infatuation which will fade with time." I shouted and withdrew my hand rudely. I left her there and moved out of the class.

When I returned, I saw that her eyes looked opaque and hollow and her face was ashen.

For the sake of the class, she was trying hard to curb her tears. I shouldn't have behaved so rudely with her. I started regretting what I had done to her but I had another thought that convinced me that my rudeness will make her hate me and it would eventually help her forget me. Thus, I left her to her condition.

That evening she did not come to coaching. I waited for her till the very end outside the coaching. I wondered if she would arrive then, she would ask me what I was doing standing outside. Everyone came but she didn't. I moved in quiet and disappointed. Coaching seemed very boring that day. Every second I kept feeling that she would arrive any moment and I would hear her voice, "*May I come in sir?*" but she didn't come. Coaching got over and we came out but there was no Naina waiting for me with her scooty. I missed her badly that day. I understood how much I had gotten addicted to her and her presence around me. I was missing her. I was remembering the past. I was remembering the times which we had spent together. My heart was cursing me for the things that I had done to her.

Next day at school, my eyes searched for her. When they found her, I breathed a sigh of relief. I saw her coming up the stairs looking very beautiful and cute. She was the same but due to the thirst in my eyes, she seemed more beautiful than before and I wanted nothing more than to keep looking at her. She came and stood in front of me and I looked at her unblinkingly.

"What are you looking at?" She didn't sound happy.

I didn't say anything but only shook my head.

"Come with me", she said and I followed her quietly to the class. She kept her bag on the desk and opened it. Her hand came out with a box, nicely wrapped in a blue gift-wrapping paper. She placed it in my hand and moved out of the class.

"Oho! gift", Ankit shouted and snatched the box from me. At that time, only the three of us were in the room.

"If it is chocolates, they're mine", Sagar said helping Ankit unwrap the gift.

"Let me see it first." I snatched the unwrapped box from them.

I opened it and found a white 'dupatta'. I got surprised. *Why had she given me that?* I took it out and a folded paper fell on the ground. Ankit picked it up.

I unfolded the 'dupatta' and the next moment I turned into stone. *Has she gone mad? How could she do this?* She had written "I love you" in her own blood. We exchanged glances but our lips were sealed. Just then the bell for the morning assembly rang but neither were we in the condition to attend it, nor did the situation allow us to.

Ankit extended that folded paper towards me. We leaned over the paper and I began to read, "Manav, I don't know why I am doing this. I am not in the right senses to judge whether it is wrong or right but this cut is does not hurt me more than your words did. You abused my love by calling it mere infatuation. I don't know why I do but I really love you. I love your cute smile. I love the way you look at me. I love to be with you, the way you look at me, the way you fight with me. I love the innocence of your eyes. You have a nice heart, Manav. The way you used to care for Shipra, the way you followed her, the way you made her feel special, I always dreamt that you'll do the same for me.

But I was wrong. I don't even blame you. You love Shipra so you can't love me, but what should I do? My heart is compelling me to do this. It beats only for you. My love is not some infatuation, Manav. I really love you and to prove my love I can sacrifice my life also. I can die for your love, Manav."

I LOVE YOU.

Below the page she used her blood again to write *I love you.* Stray drops of blood had marked both the paper and the 'dupatta'.

"She has gone mad." I said, folding the paper.

"She has gone mad or have you?" Sagar asked, "Why are you doing this to her?"

"What am I doing? What can I do? I love Shipra and she knows it." I shouted.

"You are rejecting her for that bitch!" Ankit snapped louder than me.

"Mind your language." I grabbed his collar. I could never hear the word 'bitch' for Shipra.

'*CHAT*' Ankit slapped me hard.

I left his collar and gasped. How could he have slapped me?

"You deserve this from Naina too. You are abusing her innocent love for that whore who left you." Ankit shouted.

I looked at him quietly. I could not believe that Ankit had slapped me just a second ago. Students started to fill in the class now.

"That asshole didn't care for your tears and now you don't care Naina's blood. Why am I even bothering to tell you all this? You continue to love that bitch and go to hell." I was looking at a different version of Ankit this time.

The whole class stared at us, eager to know the reason of our fighting; two people who they had never expected to argue with each other. Everyone settled down slowly. Ankit refused to sit beside me so Sagar sat between us.

I turned to look at the girls' side. Naina was sitting quietly between Megha and Sushmita, her best friends. Sadness clouded her face, the way clouds shadow the beauty of the moon. My sight slipped down from her face to her hands which were resting on the desk. When I saw her forefinger and the left wrist wrapped in white bandage, I felt as if someone had clouted my heart hard. The fact that she was sad and had hurt herself because of me hurt me a lot. Suddenly, she looked towards me and our eyes met. As she knew I was looking at her, she stole her gaze away.

The moments which we had spent together started flashing through my mind one by one. The way we met, the way we became friends, coaching, scooty driving, her proposal and the way I hurt her. I accepted that I had done wrong. I felt guilty. The thought that I had to talk to her started hammering in my head.

I should accept her proposal. I decided to fall in love with her. I decided to say 'yes' to her and it gave me goosebumps all over my body. The thought of being in a relationship, of being committed to a girl, to have a girlfriend got me very excited. My heart started beating so fast, it felt like it would jump out of my mouth. Satish sir was teaching nomenclature in chemistry but all I wanted to do was to stand up and declare my love for Naina.

As soon as Satish sir walked out of class, I went upto Naina and said, "Come with me, I want to talk something important with you."

"What do you want to say?" she asked but didn't show any motivation to move.

"Come with me, please." I tugged at her wrist and dragged her out of the class. She walked quietly parallel to me, her hand still in mine.

As we came out towards the junior wing, I saw Amit bhaiya sit-ting with the other bus-staff.

"Amit Bhaiya!" I hollered.

"HAAN BHABHI THIK HAI." He replied before I could ask him about his wife.

"Your bus is open, isn't it?" I asked him.

"Yes, Why?" he asked, despite knowing the obvious.

"We want to chill there." I said.

"With a girl?" he looked surprised and a little frightened.

"You won't be in any trouble. We will leave before the bell rings." I assured him.

"Okay, but be quick." He said.

I nodded and boarded the bus with Naina.

"Why have you brought me here? I am feeling awkward." She said.

"You are not bunking for the first time." I repeated her line to her. "There is nothing to feel awkward about." I took the window seat.

"But the bus? The small ground would have been more comfortable." She sat beside me. "If anyone sees us here , they'll assume something wide off the mark."

"Don't bother about others. No one is going to see us." I said.

"What was so important to tell me that you brought me here?"

"Why did you do this?" I took her wounded hand in mine.

"Before you deliver a long speech, I will apologise. I shouldn't have done this but at that time I had gone crazy. I was not in the condition to think right from wrong."

"It's not about the apology. Do you really love me so much that you can die for me?" I asked foolishly.

"Why? Should I have to prove it?" She asked with a smile.

"No, never. But why? I don't even love you, then why?"

"Manav, love isn't about conditions and expectations. If you love someone, you just love them whether or not you get it in return. And I could ask you the same question. Why do you love Shipra so much even when you know that she loves someone else?" I could see her affection for me stirring in her eyes.

"You are right. Love doesn't know reason, it is blind." I paused for a second and said, "Naina, your innocent love is really moving. I want to forget everything for you."

"What do you mean?" her eyes glowed with expectation.

"Naina I loved someone more than myself but she didn't care for it. I didn't get the love I wanted. This shouldn't be the case with you. You deserve the love you want."

"Really? Manav, I cannot believe my ears. It seems like I am dreaming. Tell me that I am hearing these words for real? I love you, Manav." She held my hands tightly in excitement. There was a childish glee on her face.

I smiled and patted her hair with affection. My love for her doubled when she rested her head on my shoulder. Both of us were silent. She held my right arm tightly, wrapping both her hands around it. The love in that moment, the romance of the environment was almost palpable.

Suddenly she asked, "You don't really love me, do you? You are with me only for the sake of my love towards you. Only to make me happy, isn't it?"

"PAGLI, I do. I have grown to love your innocence. I have started loving the love which you have for me. I have started loving your company. I have started loving your big attractive eyes, your lips, nose, hair, the way you talk and laugh. Everything about you is lovely for me. I can't tell you how much I missed you yesterday. When you didn't come to coaching yesterday, I felt a strange emptiness. I was incomplete and alone without you." While I was saying these words, I came so close to her that I could feel the warmth of her breath.

"If you feel so, then tell me those three magical words that I have been longing to hear for so long", she said.

Her lips shook as she was speaking and I had to curb the strong urge to kiss her rose-petal-like lips.

"Not yet. Those special words call for a special occasion."

"Then I will wait for the day when you finally say it. That day will be the best day of my life." She said with a deep sense of pleasure.

"Promise me Naina, that you will never do such a thing in future." I took her hands in mine and kissed the white bandage wrapped around her wound.

We held each other's gaze intently. Slowly I leaned in towards her. She drew closer till there was hardly any distance between our faces. She blinked twice before finally closing her eyes. Her cheeks reddened like ripe tomatoes. I felt her soft lips on mine and my lips opened automatically in response. For a few seconds our lips were locked. We were completely lost in each other.

Suddenly Shipra's face flashed across my mind.

The way I kissed her on the overbridge came to my mind and I started feeling uncomfortable. Something in me was resisting from inside. I withdrew from the kiss and sat straight. Some part of my heart was still beating for Shipra. I tried to reason with it, to replace Shipra's image with Naina's.

Naina's eyes were cast down in embarrassment. Her face was still red like the rising sun and the happiness across it shone brightly. I touched her chin and made her look at me. Our eyes met but she lowered her gaze again in shyness. She looked more beautiful when she blushed. She rested her head on my shoulder again.

"Your mom didn't ask you about this?" I took her hand in mine and stroked it softly.

"How couldn't she? Which mother wouldn't get upset on seeing her child get hurt? She didn't scold me but she wept a lot. I deeply regretted what I had done. I shouldn't have done it." Her eyes became moist.

"It's okay, babu." I wiped her tears and hugged her.

"Manav." Amit bhaiya shouted from outside.

"Yes.?" I immediately became alert.

"Come out. Alok sir will be coming soon."

Alok sir taught us English and was also the transport in charge of the school.

We came out and sneaked our way towards the class. Naina looked very happy. When we entered the class, I noticed that Shipra was staring at us. She looked unhappy with my closeness toNaina. It seemed like she wanted to talk to me but I dismissed the thought thinking that I must be mistaken.

Why would she want to talk to me now? She was happy with Pratap. I must have misunderstood her expression.

The next day, I waited for Naina in front of the

coaching. Her scooty stopped in front of me and she looked mind blowing. Each time I saw her, I found her more attractive. In her attire, a blue Kurti and black jeans, she looked like the most beautiful girl in the world.

"You are looking very beautiful" I said, mesmerised.

"Thank you", she said sheepishly.

"Don't attend coaching today."

"Why?" She asked.

"We are going somewhere else." I said.

"First, you make me bunk the class and now coaching too? You are ruining me", she smiled."Where are we going?"

"It's a secret, just come with me."

"Okay, okay." She moved towards her scooty.

"I will drive." I said.

"No, you are not safe." She said.

"ACHHA, I am not safe?" I ran to her and held her from behind. She tried her best to get rid of my hold but gave in soon.

"You are very bad", she sulked.

"Really? I don't think so." I sat on the driving seat and ignited the engine. She sat behind me.

"You're alone today? Where are your friends, Ankit and Sagar?"

"Why? Is it necessary that I always be with them?"

"No, it's not necessary, but you are rarely seen without them."

"Ankit had some work so he dropped me and left", I said, crossing the over bridge.

"Oh! Are we going to the market?" She squealed as I accelerated straight towards the 'PANCH MUHAN CHOWK'.

"Yes." I nodded.

"Where?"

"You will know when we reach there."

"No, tell me now." She was stubborn like a baby.

"Sit quietly. I won't tell", I said a little louder.

"Fine, I will keep quiet. I will not say anything. I will not talk to you anymore." She sulked like a kid. This very innocence inflamed my love for her.

She zipped her lips and sat straight, pretending to be mad. However, she couldn't even keep her word for more than five minutes and leaned into me to say,"Tell me, please? Where are we going?"

I burst into laughter. "Five minutes ago you said you are not going to talk to me anymore."

"So what?" She bumped on my back. "Fine, now I seriously won't talk to you."

I curbed my laughter and said, "My doll, talk to me." I knew that she was not going to hold her resentment for long but I wanted to pamper her and make her feel special

She pursed her lips more tightly and shook her head. I could see her in the rear view mirror.

"Okay. We are going to LAZEEZ Restaurant" I said resigned.

"Yes! I won. You had to reveal the location in order to talk to me." She chirped as if she had won some treasure.

"Yes madam, you are the winner and I am the loser." I stopped the scooty in the parking lot, in front of the restaurant.

"Always. By the way, this is my favourite restaurant", she told.

We pushed the glass doors and entered inside.

There was a table marked 'Reserved'. I pulled a chair and signalled at her to sit.

"Wow! You reserved a table for us." She sat in front of me, her face beaming with the cutest smile.

I signalled at a waiter for the menu card. He nodded

with a meaningful smile. He placed the menu card on the table and while walking back, repositioned the fan towards Naina. A bunch of small colorful chits, placed near the fan, fluttered and stroke Naina's face.

"What the hell..." Naina tried to get them out of her face but soon stopped protesting. Her eyes went to the words written on the chits. Each colorful chit had "I LOVE YOU" written on it. Naina looked at me wide eyed.

"You..." That surprise made her choke with emotion.

Her eyes were full of curiosity to know what I was going to do next. As I sat on my knees with a rose in my hand, three musicians with violins and a guitar appeared behind her. At the same time Ankit and Sagar burst balloons full of rose petals and colourful dust above her head. She was frozen in surprise. Her eyes didn't leave me for a second.

"Naina. I love you. Will you be my love?" Finally, I said those three words that she had been waiting for.

She blinked her eyes for the first time in between all that as if she had just returned from another world. Her eyes brimmed with tears threatening to fall..

I continued, "Naina, for a long time I was unaware of your love for me and when you told me about it, I didn't respect it.

I was obsessed with someone else's love at that time but your affection forced me to think differently. You cut yourself for me and I won't ever forgive myself for it. From today, I will be responsible for your happiness. I will always keep you happy and never let tears come to your eyes. I will love you more than I love myself. I am promising you now that I will only be yours. I will not think of any other girl, not even in my dreams. If you trust me then accept me, accept my love." I was still on my knees with a rose in my hands.

She took the rose from my hand and made me stand, hold-ing my arms. “Manav”, she stammered, on the verge of tears.

“You have made this day and date the most valuable in my life. I had never ever imagined that somebody would love me so much. I had always dreamt of a prince in my life who would come and make me feel like a princess. Today, I feel just like one. Today I feel like the luckiest girl in the world because you are in my life. Today, my dream have come true. I got the prince of my dreams”, she said tearfully.

“I love you, Manav. I love you.” She hugged me as tightly as she could.

The people in the restaurant started applauding us. I was secretly hoping that I had made all the girls in the restaurant jealous and all their boyfriends nervous after this master move of mine.

“I love you, BABU” She sat beside me, holding my arm tightly.

You must have friends like Ankit and Sagar with stick with you through the most difficult and amazing times of your life. The kind of friends with whom you can do anything you like and share all your feelings. These are the kind of friends who call your girlfriend ‘Bhabhi’, even before you have proposed to her.

I felt extremely lucky to have such friends as Ankit and Sagar and a girlfriend like Naina.

Before returning from the restaurant, Naina thanked Ankit and Sagar.

When I reached home, my mobile beeped to show me a message from Naina. She had written, “Today is the most cheerful day for me. I feel like I am flying in the air. My feet are not on the ground. What you have done for me, I could never hope to repay it. The way you proposed to me, I will never forget my entire life. I love you. I want to lose myself in innocence of your eyes. I want to have you in front of my eyes for the rest of my life. I don't know why I love you but I love you a lot."

"Don't be so formal. You are my princess. I will do anything for your happiness. I love you too, my sweety." I messaged her back.

The next day was Naina's birthday and I wanted to surprise her but was running out of ideas. I wanted to make is very special for her as it was her first birthday being my girlfriend. Ankit, Sagar and I sat on the banks of river KOYAL, brainstorming ways to celebrate her birthday.

"Think of something, yaar. Please." I requested both of them.

"Wish her at midnight when the clock strikes twelve", advised Sagar.

"Everybody does that, it's nothing special." Ankit interjected before I could dismiss it, myself.

Ankit knew my mind better. I needed something exciting.

"I can't think, man. I don't even celebrated my own birthday", Sagar said.

"Okay, you keep quiet. Let us think", I said and looked towards Ankit.

"Arrange a party in college and give her as many roses as her age." Ankit suggested.

I shook my head dismissively.

We passed around a lot of ideas between the three of us, but didn't approve of any of them. When an hour had passed without any conclusion, Sagar stood up annoyed and snapped "To hell with your discussion and her birthday. Even an Indo-Pak peace discussion will take less time than this. Do one thing, when the clock strikes twelve, go to her place, knock at the gate and when she comes out, wish her birthday. It will be new."

He had said those words in fury and without consequence but an idea flashed through my mind.

"What an idea, SIR JI!" I mocked, "We will go to her house."

"Her mom will chop us to pieces", Sagar retorted.

"I am not so foolish as to go inside her house. I will call her out", I said.

They looked at me muted waiting to hear what I had to say next.

"At 11 o'clock, you will come to pick me", I said looking at Ankit, "After that, we will pick up Sagar and head straight towards Naina's house together."

"I will be there", Ankit assured me. He was a true friend, always ready for whatever I asked for, without caring the least about the consequences.

"In the night and that too at midnight, I won't come." Sagar refused.

"Why?" Ankit asked.

"Midnight is the time when ghost come out." Sagar blurted.

"What?" Ankit and I stared at him in disbelief.

"What? It's true." He was utterly convinced.

"Don't worry. We will protect you. Do you see him?" Ankit pointed towards me. "He is also a ghost, going to wish his girlfriend at midnight."

"Oho! HARAMI, if I am ghost, then who are you?" I asked Ankit, grinning.

"Godfather of ghosts!" Sagar exclaimed before Ankit could reply.

"Let's go. We have to buy a cake also." I stood up, Ankit and Sagar followed me.

That night, I lay on the bed sleeplessly, waiting for Ankit. The clock showed eleven but there was no sign of him. I thought of calling him but soon decided to wait for some time. After ten minutes, I heard the roar of a bike's engine. *It must be him,* I thought and jumped off the bed and sneaked out. At the same time I got a message from Ankit which read *Come Out Fast!* Sliding past the grill of my house's gate quietly, I took my place behind him on the bike.

"Let me call Sagar, or he will never wake up." I said.

"Yes, tell him that we are reaching in five minutes", Ankit said while accelerating the bike.

When we reached Sagar's house, he was already at his gate, waiting for us in shorts and a t-shirt.

"Oye! At least wear a trouser. We are going to a girl's place", Ankit said.

"I can't! You have no idea how I have even managed to come out", Sagar retorted. His hair was all scattered.

"Fine. Just sit." I shifted forward to give him a place to sit behind me.

"No, I will sit in between." Sagar dragged me down from the bike. "

Ankit and I laughed loudly. "If a ghost comes, he will pull you out from the middle also." I took my place behind him.

Ankit rode us to Naina's house. The roads were completely deserted and the headlight threw a wide cone of brightness on the road. The quiet of the night was eerie. The silver of the moonlight and the cool November breeze of night made the roads look almost unfamiliar.

Ankit stopped the bike in front of Naina's house. It was a beautiful white bungalow surrounded by a boundary wall. The bungalow was shadowed in the dark but some light bulbs fixed on the top of the boundary wall illuminated the courtyard and the road on either side. There was a big gate at the centre of the boundary wall with a nameplate attached to the left panel, which read'*Arun Sharma*' in fancy font. That day I found out that her surname was Sharma. Everyone in class called her either just Naina or 'CHAWANNI'. I took my cell phone out from my pocket. It was ten minutes to mid-night.

I unboxed the cake and kept it on the bike seat.

"Be careful, it'll fall", Ankit yelled.

"Do one thing, pull the double stand", I said.

Ankit did as I had asked and I placed the cake on the seat, stabbing it with sixteen candles.

I had already typed and saved the message that I wanted to send Naina at midnight. I did not want to waste time typing.

As soon as the clock on my phone displayed twelve, I hit 'send' on the message that I had pre-written for her. It read, '*Happy birthday, my sweetheart. May God bless you with all the happiness in this world*'.

She responded with an immediate reply.

'*Thank you. You remembered my birthday. You are the first to wish me tonight. I am very happy Manav.*'

'*You are my baby. How can I forget your birthday? I can for-get myself, but not you.*' I texted her back.

'*By the way, can you come out.*'

'*Why? Are you outside?*'

'*Yes.*' I hit reply, excitement rising in me.

'*Don't kid me. You can't be here at this hour.*'

'*Will you come out? Don't make false assumptions.*'

'Fine, I will go out. But if you are not here, I will kill you when I see you tomorrow.' Her message illuminated the screen of my phone.

"Light the candles. She is coming", I told Ankit and Sagar.

We lit all the candles and waited for her. In a few minutes, we saw her at the gate. It appeared as if some angel was descending from the gates of heaven. She looked very cute in her pink gown. Sleep and lethargy could be seen clearly on her face. Her hair was also not tied properly but she looked very sexy.

"Happy birthday!" I stepped forward to hug her.

"Thank you", she said. When we separated, Ankit and Sagar shook her hand to wish her too.

Her face was lit with amazement with a hint of disbelief.

"Come and cut the cake now." I pulled her close to the bike and handed her the plastic knife.

She blew the candles and sliced the cake with the knife. The three of us started clapping and singing, "Happy birthday to you, Naina."

"Oye, Slow! Not so loud." Naina shushed us. "It's midnight and we are celebrating on the road."

"Okay. Okay." We sang to her softly and finishing our birthday song.

She cut a piece of cake and extended it towards me. I opened my mouth but instead of feeding it to me, she rubbed the slice on my face.

"Oho! You want to play with me?" I reached for another piece of cake. When she guessed my intention, she tried to run away but I held her by the waist and pulled her close to me and then rubbed the piece of cake on her face.

"Bravo man! Bravo!" Ankit shouted excitedly.

"Oho! Bravo?" Naina threw a piece of cake at his face.

"It's not fair that you remain clean alone." Ankit rubbed a piece of cake on Sagar's face too. All of us started laughing. Not a single piece of cake went inside out mouths. We wasted the whole cake rubbing or throwing it at each other.

"Don't spoil my dress", shouted Naina. "Or it'll become difficult for me to explain it to mom in the morning."

When the whole cake was finished, Naina thanked Ankit and Sagar again. She then came to me, held my hand and said, "Thank you, Manav. Thank you for making my birthday so special. Why didn't you come to my life earlier? I wasted sixteen birthdays without you. I love you, Manav. I love you." She hugged me tight. "Promise me that you'll never leave me and that you'll always be with me, that you will love me like this forever. Promise me, Manav."

I stroked her hair affectionately and said, "You are my life, Naina. How can I leave you? You are as much a part of me as breathing. I'd much sooner stop breathing than leave you. I love you."

"Oye! LAILA-MAJNU, it's almost 2 A.M.", Ankit scoffed at us.

We separated and waved each other good-bye.

The next day at school, Naina walked towards us with a big smile on her face. The three of us were standing in the garden looking at the commerce section girls.

"What happened? Why are you smiling like that?" I asked.

"When mom came to drop me off at the bus stop, she saw the cake smeared on the road and and had asked '*Who has thrown away so much cake like this?*'"

"What did you tell her?" Ankit asked.

"I said 'PAGALO KI KAMI THODI NA HAI'(There is no lack of mad men here.)" She laughed.

"Are we crazy?" I smacked her head gently.

The festive season was going on. After *Rakshabandhan*, *Dussehra* and *Deepawal*i, it was time for 'CHHATH PUJA'.

It is a three day festival which includes a holy bath on the first day, fasting and the '*Araghya*' offering of water to the setting sun on the second day followed by *Kheer Bhojan* and the offering of cow milk and fruits and *Thekua* to the rising sun the third day.

My mother was participating in the 'CHHATH PUJA' that year. There were two main venues for 'CHHATH PUJA' in our city. One was river 'KOYAL' and the other was river 'AMANAT'. On that occasion, the whole of Daltonganj could be seen gathered at one of those two placed. It was our favorite festival. We waited eagerly for the day to go to the rivers as it was a good place to checkout girls. All the beautiful faces of our city could be seen there on those two days.

It was the evening of the second day of 'CHHATH PUJA' and we were getting ready to go to the river. We groomed ourselves quite well too, in order to impress the girls. We preferred to go to river 'AMANAT' because it was in the outskirts of the city, hence was more spacious and cleaner than river 'KOYAL'.

We were preparing to go when I messaged Naina, '*We are going to AMANAT. Where are you?*'

'*AMANAT*' My mobile beeped to show her message.

'*Okay, see you there.*' I replied.

'*Will you be able to find me in that crowd?*' I got her message.

'*Absolutely. I will look through each and every 'GHAT' till I find you. By the way, which color'd dress will you be wearing?*' I thought it would be easy to search for her if I knew what she was wearing.

'*Pink top and blue jeans.*' I punched the button of my mobile to see her message.

'*Okay, bye. I have a lot of work to do here.*' She sent another quick text.

'*How late you will be reaching there?*' I quickly sneaked in a last text.

'*About an hour. We are about to leave.*' She replied.

'*Okay. Bye. We are also leaving.*' I kept the phone in

my pocket.

"Why don't you enter inside that mobile?" Papa shouted angrily. "Hundreds of tasks are pending here and you are playing with that devil's device. Come here." He yelled from the PUJA room where my mother sat with other women of the neighborhood, singing 'CHHATH' songs.

"I am here." I went to stand next to my father the next moment.

"Tie these sugarcane on the top of the car." He indicated towards a bunch kept aside in the room.

I tied the sugarcane above the BOLERO which we had rented to go to the river and back.

"Carry this holy 'DAURA'", Papa said and helped me put that heavy basket containing all the PUJA material, on my head.

My mother marched out with her hands joined in prayer, followed by all the other women singing sweet CHHATH songs. My father and I followed close behind with the 'DAURA' on my head. Everyone settled inside the car and we were soon off.

When we reached the main road, it was jammed with other PUJA vehicles with sugarcane tied the roof of the cars, like every year. As we reached the over-bridge near AMANAT, we found a huge traffic jam blocking the entrance of the river. Every car played a different CHHATH PUJA song, creeping inch by inch towards the river.

After about an hour, we managed to reach the river. Policemen on duty directed the vehicles for efficient parking.

The whole party proceeded towards the ghat that we had prepared the previous day. The DAURA was placed on my head again. The soft sands of the riverbank felt like silky cotton spread below our feet to welcome us and other devotees. The riverbank looked lively and festive with the men, women and children that had arrived there in colourful clothes.

I helped my mother set up the PUJA installation with the sugarcane and the DURGA mural. When everyone had settled, I told papa, "I am going to have a stroll in the water."

"Okay but return on time before the sun sets. 'ARAGHYA LENA HOGA'", Papa said. While devotees offered ARA-GHYA, we touched the holy water or milk to our heads in respect.

I folded my jeans up to my knees and entered the river. The cold water relieved my feet of the tiredness of the whole day. The shallow water seemed to jump about my feet in delight as I took one step after the other. I started walking in the water, my eyes searching for Naina.

After passing a couple of GHATs, I saw Naina's mother in a red saree, sitting behind a sugarcane. I looked for Naina around that ghat, but was unsuccessful. I suddenly saw Ankit walking towards me. The friend trumped the lover this time!

"Oye! Where is your GHAT?" I shook his hand.

"Back there…" he indicated behind him, where his father was standing.

"Is your father performing CHHATH PUJA?" I asked.

"Yes. Papa and Mummy both", he replied.

"Your father had scammed a lot from S.S Hospital. He can't attain absolution just by performing CHHATH PUJA." Suyash appeared from behind him and interfered in our conversation.

He was our only friend from the commerce section in school. Ankit's father was a doctor at S.S Hospital and Suyash never missed a chance to make fun of it.

"I never go to S.S Hospital," He continued to pull Ankit's leg.

"Why?" I asked.

"KIDNEY NIKAL LETA HAI ISKA BAAP(His father steals the patients' kidneys.)", he laughed and I joined him.

"Yes, he will take out yours' too." Ankit retorted.

"That's why I don't go to your father. I love my kidney." Suyash laughed out louder.

Ankit contorted his face into a grimace. Someone called for Suyash and left.

We walked all the way to the last GHAT but we didn't find Naina. We returned to check other side when we saw Naina walking towards us. She was hovering like a butterfly with her friends Sushmita and Kriti. In her pink top and blue jeans she looked the most beautiful amongst all the girls present there.

"Hi! Looking gorgeous!" I exclaimed as we drew close to each other.

"Thank you, but I can't talk to you right now. The whole town is staring at us."

She was right. I didn't want to get caught indulging with her myself.

We moved towards different directions. The environment at the river bank was light and festive. People was enjoying the water and the sun-set, talking to each other and taking pictures. Ankit and I clicked some photographs too. We missed Sagar. He went to Koyal River with his family because it was closer to his house.

We reached the other end of the bank under the bridge where I halted in my steps with a pleasant surprise. I saw Shipra playing in the water with some of her friends. She was in a black top and dark blue jeans. The black color accentuated the fairness of her skin. *How could one look so beautiful and cute!* She took some water in the palm of her hand and threw it towards Richa. Richa tried to shield herself at first but soon gave in and proceeded to do the same to her. Ruchi, who was standing away, started throwing water on both of them. A smile appeared on my face, seeing them play like kids.

What is this Punjabi girl doing here? I thought, my eyes fixed on her face.

Suddenly her eyes met with mine and she stood straight. We froze like statues. Her friends continued to throw water at her but she didn't care anymore. We looked at each other unblinkingly, as if searching for something. I don't know what attraction she held in her eyes, but I felt like going to her and telling her that she was the most beautiful girl in the world and that I loved her more than anything else. My mind interjected at the same time, reminding me that she loved someone else and that I had promises to keep with Naina.

I came out of my reverie when Ankit tapped me on my shoulder saying, "The sun is setting. It's time for 'ARGHYA'".

Shipra continued to look at me. It seemed like her eyes were trying to tell me something but Ruchi tugged at her hand and pulled her away. I returned to my GHAT.

Do I still love her? I asked myself but a voice in my head answered, "No, you don't love her, you love Naina."

My heart was in disagreement, "If you don't love her, then why do you feel so strongly for her? Why were you frozen a second ago on seeing her? What did you look so deep into her eyes? Why did you not feel good when Ruchi pulled her away?"

Before my heart could ask more questions, my mind screamed, "Why are you even thinking about all this? She belongs to someone else. She loves someone else and you love Naina. You have made promises to her." My heart kept quiet. My mind had won.

I reached my GHAT. My mother had taken her position in the water, facing the setting sun.

"Go and call the priest for the 'ARGHYA'", Papa instructed.

"Okay." I moved towards another GHAT where a priest was pouring water down a sieve held by a devotee. The people standing around her placed their hands below that sieve to collect the holy water in their cupped palms.

"PANDIT JI, please come for the ARGHAY." I requested the priest after accepting ARAGHYA there.

He charged a hundred and fifty rupees just for pouring water at us. After the ARGHAYA, we started packing up the things to go home. Some people had arranged to stay at the river side the whole night but we decided to come back in the morning before sunrise to follow up with the ceremonies of the next day.

At three 'o'clock, I messaged Naina, '*When are you leaving for the river?*'

I got a reply an hour later when we had already left the house. '*We will be late. Still need half an hour.*'

'*We are on the way already. See you there.*' I messaged her.

We reached in the river bank, placed the sugarcane on the GHAT and settled down. I went to the Naina's GHAT but they hadn't come yet.

The sky started to grow pale and the horizon started to redden, in anticipation of the sun. Devotees had started entering the river to make the offering but there was no sign of Naina's family. I was waiting eagerly for her. I didn't go towards the bridge again for the fear of seeing Shipra again. Her face made all my repressed feelings and emotions to come out.

My mother stood up to enter the river. I grew tense in anticipation for Naina. Soon enough, I saw her with her family rushing hurriedly towards the GHATs. I entered the river right behind my mother. My happiness surpassed all limits when I saw that Naina's mother came to stand right beside my mother. Naina and I exchanged a happy glance.

Suddenly a woman from Naina's side squealed, "Naina, where is the milk?"

"It must be in the 'DAURA'." Naina yelled back and ran towards her GHAT to search for it herself.

After some time they returned with perplexed faces.

"Mummy, I think I forgot the pot of milk at home." Naina said lamenting.

"KYA KARE HUM IS LADKI KA?" Her mother slapped her forehead, "The whole day you are lost in your mobile phone, how can one expect you to remember things?"

"You forgot the milk?" My mother asked them.

"Yes, due to this PAGLI." Naina's mother nodded sheepishly.

"Don't curse her. It happens sometimes. We have more than enough milk, please accept half of it. How cute is your daughter! Please don't scold her." My mother extended the pot of milk towards her and poured half of it into their pot.

"Don't be deceived by her face. She is more wicked than she looks", an aunt from her side said and made everyone laugh.

"Go find a PANDIT JI", Papa asked me.

"What's the need? We have our own priest here. While we are preparing our offering, he can pour the ARGHAY for you." Naina's mother said, looking towards their priest.

"Yes, why not?" The PANDIT JI smiled.

Before he could pour our ARGHAY, Naina's mother recognised my face and said, "You are the same boy who was involved in the accident with Naina?"

"Yes aunty." I smiled.

"Accident? Where? " My mummy asked concerned.

Naina's mother told her about the incident and soon they started talking as if they had known each other for years.

I leaned towards Naina and whispered in her ear, "Our families are bonding well. Get ready to be the bride now."

"Be quiet." She slapped me affectionately.

After the PUJA, we proceeded towards our respective vehicles, our mothers exchanged warm greetings and kind invitations to each of their houses.

Winter passed away before we knew it. Everything comes to an end, just like our academic year as well as our school life. Our farewell day was drawing close and we dealt with it with mixed feelings. We were excited for the party but quite sad too for our school years were about to come to an end.

The dress code for boys was formals and for girls, sari. A day before the farewell, Ankit and Sagar came to my house an hour before the event was about to start. Ankit wore a black suit and Sagar, a fancy blue shirt with black trousers.

"Let's go." I came out in a formal white shirt and dark grey trousers.

"What is this? You look like a simple-ton!" Sagar exclaimed.

"Do you want me to put lipstick and eyeliner on my face?" Ankit and I laughed.

"'GAWAR'. Let me help you." Sagar applied some hair gel on my head and fashioned them into spikes.

"It looks like I got an electric shock." I said, looking in the mirror.

"You look different. Let it be like this. It's the trend now." Ankit approved of my hair style.

The three of us got on the bike and Ankit accelerated towards the school, however he stopped the bike at RED-MA near the wine shop before taking the final turn towards our campus.

"Are you nuts? Will you drink today, at our farewell?" I wasn't in favor of drinking that day.

"Today is the happiest day of our lives. We are going to be free from this prison we call our school. If we don't drink today, when will we find the opportunity again?" Ankit bellowed excitedly. Ankit called the same school 'prison', which I was so sad leaving.

"But we don't have the time to go drinking. Where will we drink?" I asked.

"In school", Ankit said.

"What?!" Sagar and I looked at him in surprise. "Are you crazy? How can you take these bottles to school?" I asked.

"We won't. I will transfer the beer to soft-drink bottles", Ankit said proudly.

"You are really a big bastard", Sagar sighed.

We bought three bottles of beer and transferred the contents to two soft-drink bottles and took them to school.

We were the last people from our batch to arrive at the scene. Everyone looked cheerful and enthusiastic, busy gossiping, meeting, exchanging numbers and taking photos together. We clicked a few pictures too before we heard the voice of Ajay sir on the microphone, "Class twelfth, please take your seat. Your farewell is about to begin."

After three announcements and twenty minutes, we finally settled down. A junior came to the stage and delivered the welcome speech. He thanked us on behalf of the whole class for what they had learned from us and shared some memories of when we as seniors helped them. He expressed how sad they were that they won't see us in the school anymore and that they'll try and fulfil all responsibilities, being the new seniors of the school after us. After his speech, the cultural program started with a song "EK DIN AAP YUN HMKO MIL JAYENGE…." and Bhavna sung it really well.

Ankit extended the bottle containing beer towards me and we started sipping while enjoying the program. The alcohol slowly started to show its effect and made us react overtly to the smallest of things. We started laughing and shouting and whistling despite Ajay Sir's repeated instructions to maintain discipline. The fact that it was our last day at school, gave us more courage to do mischief.

When Rima came to the stage to dance on 'SHEELA KI JAWANI', the three of us stood and started dancing with our chairs raised high above, in our hands. Following us, half the boys started dancing the same way.

Seeing our nonsense, Ajay sir came to the stage and an-nounced angrily, "We warned you repeatedly but it's too late now. Due to your undisciplined behavior, we are postponing the program. You can now proceed towards the food stalls and then you are free to go home. Your farewell is over. No batch had ever behaved as badly as you have today."

Some students were disappointed by the news but most of us scattered happily and resumed taking pictures and exchanging numbers and making promises to keep in touch.

"Manav, come here." I heard Naina's voice and turned towards her. She was clicking pictures with Sushmita, Megha and Kriti.

The three of us reached them and exchanged greetings.

My gaze were stuck on Naina. Due to my drunken state, I had failed to notice her earlier, but now I looked at her carefully. She could beat an angel in her blue sari. Her matching long earrings were accentuating her appeal for me.

"Are you all drunk?" Naina sniffed alcohol on me.

"A little", I used my thumb and forefinger to indicate a small amount.

"We were celebrating our farewell so....", Ankit grinned.

"Celebrating with alcohol, nothing can correct your ways", Naina slapped playfully on my arm.

I smiled and pulled her close, "Ankit click some pictures of us."

We got busy snapping pictures when I saw Shipra coming towards me. She looked like an Indian diva in her pink sari. Her slim waist appeared even more petite in a sari and her bosom appeared even more ample in her blouse. She looked so sexy and appealing that a man could have sacrifice his life to get her.

"Hi", Shipra cooed.

The pink of her lipstick seemed to invite me to lick it but the little trace of sanity that I had at that point, restrained me. I replied with a smile, "Hello! How are you?"

"Fine." She smiled back at me and said, "I want to snap some pictures with you. We are separating today. God knows when we'll meet again? I will keep these photos with me as a memory."

"Shipra, are you separating from Manav only? Don't you want to keep our photos as memory too?" Ankit teased her.

"No, that's not it. I will click pictures with you also."

She said sheepishly, her face red with embarrassment.

She clicked some pictures with me and some in the group. She made sure she stood next to me in every picture we took. While she was with me, everything looked cheerful and happy. Her presence filled every pore of my body with happiness.

After a while, she said, "Okay, bye. I am going now. You all enjoy."

Her words '*I am going*' really miffed me. I had forgotten that she had to go too. She was not mine to have. She had come to say good bye. She had come in my life and near me that day, only for some time. Not forever.

"Where are you going?" Words automatically slipped out of my mouth.

"Home, it's getting late so...", she said and turned around. I caught a shadow of sadness on her face too before she left.

All happiness seemed to have been sucked away, as soon as she left. My face grew dim with the thought that she was gone from my life forever and that I would never see her again. My heart beat in protest and my eyes swam with tears that I wiped secretly. The school, the party, the people had all lost their cheer. I said goodbye to Naina and came out of the school with Sagar and Ankit.

Hospital again

* * *

After class twelve, I never saw Shipra again. She went to Delhi University to Pratap's college, which I found out about through her Facebook posts. She had uploaded pictures with Pratap and had made posts about her new college. I blocked her after seeing those pictures because I could not bear to see her with someone else.

Naina and I went to Ranchi to prepare for IITJEE but failed to qualify the exam; we took admission in a private engineering college. I decided to take admission in Delhi with the hope that I'll run into Shipra one day. Naina followed me to the same college. We spent three years together but thoughts of Shipra still invaded my mind in moments of loneliness. I had begun to forget her but seeing her after all those years, reopened some old wounds.

My chain of though broke when Shipra started murmuring in her semi-conscious state. The nurse and I looked at her but couldn't understand a word. I looked towards the nurse.

"She is coming into her senses", the Nurse replied.

"Papa… papa." There were the first words that she uttered clearly. I pulled my stool closer to the bed and took her hand into mine. She gripped it tightly.

"Papa, I am alone papa. He betrayed me." She murmured.

Her murmurs were dispersed with long stretches of silence. She kept calling for her father, tears streaming down her eyes.

Seeing her condition, my throat got chocked too. *What had happened to her? Why did she say she was alone? Who had betrayed her? Had Pratap betrayed her or was it someone else?* I had a lot of questions, but the only person who could answer them was lying unconscious in front of me.

"Manav", suddenly she called my name.

"Yes, Shipra." I thought she had come to her senses and had recognized me. I leaned closer but her eyes were still shut.

"Manav, Manav…", she murmured again.

I felt elated thinking that I still occupied a place in her mind, however unconscious.

"Manav, where have you gone? Why did you leave me?" I couldn't believe my ears. "I am alone without you, Manav." She continued murmuring. I had never expected that she would still have such feelings in her heart for me.

"Manav, where have you gone? I love you, Manav. I love you from bottom of my heart." I heard the words that I had been waiting to hear forever. Here I was in a hospital with Shipra badly wounded in front of me. I did not imagine to hear these words in this condition. Shipra could be the only girl who proposed to her beloved in a hospital, lying unconscious, without even knowing that she was confessing her feelings.

My heart started to beat fast. The hand with which I was holding Shipra's hand started shaking. Someone has correctly said, 'First love is always the first. It runs in your veins. You can't separate yourself from it even of you want to.' I got up from the stool to sit next to her on the bed and started stroking her hair affectionately. Suddenly, she stopped murmuring and opened her eyes, blinking repeatedly. She took a while to absorb the situation and place she was in, and exclaimed, "How did I come here? Who brought me here?" She must have remembered her accident.

Suddenly her eyes caught my face and she froze. She took a few seconds to look and me, perhaps to confirm that it was indeed I, in front of her eyes. Her face regained some color and she tried to sit up straight. She leaned forward to hold me and said, "Where had you been, Manav? Why had you left me alone?" She held me so tight as if she feared I would leave if she slackened her grip. "You can't imagine how much I have missed you? I love you Manav, I love you." She came to the realisation of our situation and separated herself from me. Her eyes were cast down and she was blushing profusely. She coughed twice in awkwardness. I extended a glass of water towards her which she held without looking at me. The confession might have made her blush but perhaps she did not remember that she had said those words to me before.

"How are you feeling now?" I tried to break the silence.

Before she could answer me, the doctor entered with the nurse and asked her the same question.

"Fine", she cooed.

The doctor examined her and turned to me. "She is fine now. For today, we will keep her under observation. Tomorrow you can take her home."

"Okay doctor. Thank you", I said.

"We are leaving now. If you have any problem, call for the nurse."

After they had left, I was left alone in the room with

Shipra. We sat quietly for some time, stealing quite glances at each other and waiting for the other to start speaking.

"Why did you save me, Manav? Why didn't you leave me to die?" She was on the verge of tears.

This startled me. *What was she saying*? I had saved her life and instead of thanking me, she chided me.

"Why are you talking like this?" I looked at her surprised.

"I said nothing wrong, Manav. Girls like me deserve to die."

"What has happened, Shipra? Please tel me."

"I am ruined Manav. He ruined me." She supported herself up on the pillow. "I would prefer death over a life like this."

Tears started rolling down her cheeks.

Watching her cry made me feel like someone was squeezing my heart. "What happened, Shipra? Babu? Why are you crying?" I walked close to her.

The force of my affection broke the barrier of her tears and shame. She clung to me and started sobbing like a baby. "Why did you leave me, Manav? Why did you leave me alone?"

"Don't cry, baby. Please be quiet." I stroked and patted her back gently. "I had never left you Shipra. I was always there for you."

I continued to console her but her weeping did not stop. The cloth over my shoulder got soaked with her tears. After a while she sat back and sobbed, "You were not with me. You had left me."

I wiped her tears affectionately and said, "No, you told me that you didn't love me. You love someone else." I totally forgot about Naina at that time. Naina meant everything for me and I didn't have any feelings left for Shipra, until that moment. I couldn't understand why I was unable to control myself. I forgot all the promise which I'd made to Naina. I had promised her that I won't ever look at another girl as long as she was with me, but here I was losing my hear over Shipra again. I knew it was wrong but I was unable to stop myself. Shipra seemed to have bewitched me.

"I told you to go and you just went away. You did not turn back once to see how I was doing without you? You have no idea of my loneliness. You didn't bother to check once if I was happy or not. If you had, I would have surrendered myself to you." A drop of tear shone like a pearl at the corner of her eye.

"Where is Pratap?" I was curious to know about him and their relationship.

As soon as she heard his Pratap, her face contorted with hatred.

"Don't take his name, Manav. His name stings me." She shout-ed. "He is a wild wolf who destroyed my life and burned all my dreams and happiness away. He left my world in ashes." Her eyes got moist with fresh tears.

I couldn't understand why she had such resentment for him? Perhaps they broke up for some reason and Shipra now accused him for various mistakes. I felt secretly exhilarated, seeing such hatred in her eyes for him .

"What are you saying? What happened between the two of you", I asked curiously.

"Don't say both. I have been at the receiving end of all things bad." She spluttered.

"Please don't cry. Tell me what happened? I really want to know. Why are you crying? Please tell me", I begged her to confess.

"What happened today was not an accident, Manav. I tried to commit suicide."

I was stunned. "What!? What are you saying?

Suicide?" I was in deep disbelief.

"It's a long story, you don't want to indulge in it." She wiped her tears but more streamed down her eyes..

"I want to indulge. Please tell me." I was almost yelling.

"People say that sorrows half when you share them, but the tragedy of my life is such that I can't even share it with anyone. But I will share it with you, not because you are forcing me to, but because I trust you. I hope you will support and understand me" she said.

"I am always with you." I gently stroked her hair.

"When you fought with me on the stairs the first time, you seemed like a wild and misbehaved boy. When you first started staring at me, I got very irritated but slowly started liking it. I started noticing whether you were looking at me or not. I became habitual of your gaze. If you looked at someone else, I felt bad. Before I could give this feeling time to grow I caught you checking my bag and creating mischief with my things. I decided never to talk to you again but then you saved me from Ajay Sir and introduced me to Volleyball. I had never played the game before, but you motivated me. It helped me to get to know you better too. You were friendly, funny, romantic and interesting, completely different from what I had thought of you. My heart was convinced that there could be no guy better than you. I again started feeling for you. I started liking you. Not just liking, I started loving you." She stammered twice while saying the last sentence. "But I kept waiting for you to make the move", she added.

"Why didn't you confess your feelings to me yourself?" I intervened.

Tears welled her eyes again. "How could I? If a girl expressed her feelings of love, the society labels her shameless. So I curbed my feelings and waiting for you to approach me, but you didn't. And then I met Pratap."

I did not want to discuss their relationship in detail, but I allowed her to continue.

"I was deeply attracted towards him and it was very good in the beginning. I felt like we were made for each other. I was very happy to finally have love in my life. But with time, our conversations started to turn towards sex. I assumed it was common in every relationship and didn't care much about it. Then he started talking about sex all the time. He started forcing me to send pictures of my body."

"What?" I exclaimed.

"Yes. He argued that he was my lover and had the right to see my body. According to him, it was only fair in love. But how could I reveal my modesty to a guy whom I had met only a few times. I tried to make him understand but he was not ready to listen. And we started fighting over small things. The love between us started to fade. Then I started missing the way you used to care for me, the way you used to stare at me, the way you used to follow me. I missed your friendship and affection for me. I realized then that no one could be better than you. No one could love me more than you. Pratap had never loved me. He had only used me for my body. When I finally felt the depth of your love, I decided to tell you, to confess my feelings to you but I noticed that your attention had shifted to Naina. You did not look at me anymore. You did not take interest in me anymore. You never followed me home, nor were you eager to talk to me. You had started to ignore me. You were always with Naina", she said enviously.

I didn't interrupt her and she continued, "I can't explain how bad I felt when I you with her but it seemed like you had decided to hurt me, to take revenge on me. You left playing volley ball. You starting taking tuition classes with her too and the day when you left with her on her scooty, I felt like a bullet had hit my heart. I was helpless. I could do nothing but to see you and love you silently. The day you accepted her proposal, all my hopes and expectations shattered into pieces. I was disappointed but I didn't stop loving you. You were always in my heart. I missed you every minute of my life. That's why I came to you for taking pictures at the farewell. I didn't have anything to remember you by so I clicked some pictures with you. Facebook was the only way to stay connected with you but you had blocked me there too. Why had you blocked me?" she asked.

"I saw your college pictures with Pratap and decided to keep my distance from you, thereon." I told her the truth.

"Yes. That was the biggest mistake of my life. I gave him another chance. I trusted him again. After the result of class twelfth came out, he called to ask my score and advised me to take admission in his college which was in Delhi University. I always dreamed of studying in D.U. so I agreed. Pratap grew close to me again and succeeded to convince me that all the problems in our relationship were due to long distance. He assured me that since we were together, nothing would go wrong. But he started messing with me again. Whenever he found me alone, he tried to touch me unnecessarily. He used to force me to go for movies with him and in the darkness tried to feel my private parts. He soon started convincing me for sex with examples of other girls who readily got intimate with guys. I refused straight away. I was a small town girl from a middle class family. I had nothing but my honour to my credit. We started fighting again, but I never agreed to do what he wanted. How could I forget my parents and the values they gave me? When he failed to get my body through love, he stooped to the lowest level imaginable and revealed his true ugly face."

"What do you mean? What did he do to you?" I asked.

Shipra wiped her tears but her eyes did not remain dry even for a moment. "There was this girl, Neha, whom I met through Pratap. She was very nice, silent and a little reserved. Slowly we became good friends. One day, she came to my hostel and asked me to go with her to her flat. I had gone to her flat at an earlier occasion too so I didn't question her when she asked me to go this time. When I entered in her room, I saw Pratap sitting there with a friend. I knew the other guy, I had seen him on a previous occasion with Pratap. He was Sandeep Gurjar, a rotten rich kid. His father was the regional president of the ruling party. His father's political influence had made him arrogant and criminal. He was a drug addict and was a bad influence on Pratap."

"What were they doing at Neha's house?" I interrupted Shipra.

"Waiting for me with evil intentions." Her eyes welled up again.

"What evil intentions?" I did not like where the story was headed.

"Sandeep stood up and locked the door. I was frightened and asked him the reason for it. I looked towards Neha and asked her, '*what is this Neha? Have you brought me here for this?*' She didn't reply and went inside her room. I was left alone in the dinning area with those two boys. I felt hopeless and my mind froze. I wanted to shout but my voice drowned somewhere inside me. I felt a strange heaviness and a wave of nausea hit me. Before I could think, Pratap gripped me from behind and tied my mouth with my own 'DUPATTA.' I requested, pleaded, even gripped their feet in request but they didn't listen. They raped me over and over. They ruined my life." She started sobbing loudly.

I was frozen with pain and dread for her. How could anyone be so wild, cruel and inhuman. I wrapped her in my arms, "Don't cry. Everything will be fine. I am with you. You're safe now. Please be calm." I couldn't help my tears either as they leaked out of my eyes. "Why didn't you complain to the police?"

"While one guy was exploiting me, the other was shooting the whole thing in his mobile. They threatened to release the video on Youtube and Facebook if I went to the police", she continued to sob. "What can I do now? I can't even share my sorrow with anyone. With the threat to upload that video, they summoned me twice to a hotel and exploited me again. Tell me, what choice did I have besides suicide? I raced my scooty towards your car without knowing that it was you driving it."

I couldn't stop crying, thinking about the mental stress that Shipra must be going through, the pain which had made her prefer death over life.

She hid herself in my arms which I wrapped more tightly around her. Perhaps she felt safer now, having unburdened herself with the secret that was killing her. She wanted my help and I had to do something for her.

When she calmed down I asked to her, "Didn't you ask Neha why she did that to you?"

Instead of answering me, she extended her mobile towards me.

It had a text from Neha. '*I am sorry Shipra. Please forgive me. I have done the worst with you but I didn't do it willingly. I was under compulsion. I used to be Sandeep's girlfriend. Once on his birthday, he convinced me to come to his house. Pratap was there too and they did the same with me what they have done to you. They made a video of it and now I am like a puppet for them. Please forgive me.*'

"What? This is outrageous!" I hit the wall angrily.

Shipra wept holding my arms and I sat quietly next to her. I couldn't understand what to do next? The doctor came in to examined her again and gave her leave to go. I dropped her to her hostel and then returned to my own hostel. I was in the third year of engineering then. The car had belonged to my senior from whom I promised to buy it when he left college. I handed over the keys to him and collapsed on my bed. I started thinking about Shipra, and after an hour, made up my mind about a plan of action. I took out my mobile from the pocket and called Shipra.

"Hello." I heard Shipra's groggy voice.

"Yes, its Manav." I said. "Are you sleeping?" "Yes" she replied.

"Please wake up and listen carefully", I said. "You have to complain to the police" I said firmly.

"But what will happen to me?" she asked.

"Nothing will happen to you." I assured her.

"What if they will upload the video?" she asked scared.

"Let them upload whatever they want. I am with you. You have to take action Shipra."

"But if the video..." she started but I interrupted her.

"Why are you so frightened of the video? If you don't complaint they will continue calling you. Are you ready to become a slave to them? And it's not just about you. If you leave these animals free in the society, they will exploit many other girls. Who knows how many innocent girls they are blackmailing just like you and Neha. You have to take the bullet and send them behind bars in order to save other girls like yourself." I tried to convince her.

"But what about my future? Who will marry me after knowing the whole truth about me?" She said tearfully.

"I will marry you, Shipra. There is still a lot of love

in my heart for you. I will be always with you." I assured her.

I had agreed to marry her without thinking about Naina. *Was it because I still loved Shipra?* I adored Naina but Shipra was my first love. I had almost erased all memories of Shipra from my heart but I agreed to marry her in a second. I don't know what moved me, but it was *something like love*, which compelled me to betray Naina.

"Thanks Manav. I have loved you throughout my life, now you know. If you are by my side, I can fight the whole world. I am ready to complain against them." She sounded confident and determined.

We decided to meet the next morning and go to the police station together.

The police station in-charge was very good to us. He listened to our statement carefully and then asked Shipra to give her statement in written. The inspector then said, "Don't worry. I am not going to let them off easy. But you have to be firm on your statement. Tomorrow you'll have to come for a medical checkup whetheror not you have been assaulted. Alright?"

"Yes sir, we will come tomorrow." I replied before Shipra could say anything.

The next day at ten in the morning, I reached in front of Shipra's hostel. Shipra came down and took her place behind me on my bike. I was about to start when another bike stopped beside me with two boys our age. I recognised one of them as Pratap. I immediately grew alert but unfortunately was too late.

The boy sitting behind Pratap yelled angrily at Shipra, "Did you think you'll complain to the police, ruin our life and we will let you go?" and threw some kind of liquid at Shipra's face. She tried to shield herself but failed. The acid stung her skin and she fell from the bike with a painful yelp. She squirmed on the road in pain but soon her protests ended and she lost consciousness. Pratap and his friend fled the scene.

I was frozen in shock. I bent next to her, shook her repeatedly and called out her name but she did not respond. The left side of her face was acid-burnt and bleeding. I filled with such desperation and longing that I had never felt before. My heart ached for her. My eyes were blinded by tears and I could barely manage to keep myself from fainting too. People from the nearby shops had gathered around us. With their help, I managed to take her to the hospital.

The Doctor said that he had started the treatment but since it was a police case, the authorities were to be informed immediately. I called Naina and told her everything. She arrived at the hospital in twenty minutes. Tears hadn't stopped rolling down my eyes all morning. She drew close to me, wiped my tears and said, "Don't worry. Everything will be fine."

I hugged Naina tightly. I felt completely helpless and wanted a shoulder to rest my head on and weep. I found that in Naina. I sobbed, "They threw acid on her face in front of me, Naina. I couldn't to do anything. They ruined her in front of me."

"Don't worry. It's not your fault." She tried to calm me down.

When I regained some strength and sat straight, she asked, "Have you called her parents?"

"Not yet." I said.

"You should call them."

I had Shipra's bag with me. I took out her mobile and called her father. I told him that Shipra had met with an accident and that she was under treatment at Shree Ram Hospital. He tried to ask how and where but I hung up. I didn't have the strength to tell him anymore.

Very soon, media people and news reporters started filtering in and asked me several questions. Women's welfare committee and political leaders from various parties also gathered there. They announced that they were going to hold a protest against the government at Ramleela Maidan because the government was unable to prevent such accidents.

Shipra was shifted to her ward. Her left cheek was covered in white bandage. She lay unconscious and I sat next to her, stroking her hair affectionately. *How unlucky she was! Within a week, she had been forced to lie on a hospital bed twice.* Naina sat beside me too.

At mid-night, Shipra came to her senses. She murmured and called out for her father and me again in the semi-conscious state of her mind. When she came to her senses, she took her hand to the left side of her face and felt the thick bandage on it. Tears started rolling down her cheeks.

"They ruined my face, Manav. What wrong had I done to them? Why did they do this? Why did I do to deserve this?" She wept holding my hand.

"Please don't cry Shipra. It's not your fault. You deserve nothing of it. Please calm down." Tears streamed down my face too. Naina's eyes were also wet.

"Are you still ready to marry this ugly version of me?" she asked sobbing.

Naina turned to me surprised but said nothing.

"Yes Shipra, I will marry you. I am always going to be with you."

Naina's face lost all colour and became clouded with sadness. She got up and left the room.

"I'll come back in a minute, Shipra." I followed Naina out of the ward.

I found Naina crying outside. I kept a hand on her

shoulder from behind her.

"Why did you do this to me?" she sobbed. "If you have always loved Shipra, why did you pretend to love me?"

"Naina, I am not in love with Shipra. I love you, but you see her condition, don't you? If I won't marry her, nobody will."

"How are you the only person to think of this? Please don't do this to me."

"Naina, you can easily find any good man to be with you, and he'll be lucky to have you but who will marry Shipra after all that has happened to her? Please forgive me, but I can't leave her like this." I said firmly.

"If you have made up your mind then I have nothing left to say. All the best. You are really great to be ready to accept Shipra after all this; it proves that my choice was not wrong. I will always love you. Shipra was your first love and now you have her. I hope you are happy." She walked away from the hospital with tears in her eyes.

I went back to the ward to take my seat next to Shipra and took her hands in mine.

"Sorry Manav, I came between Naina and you", she said sadly.

"It's not what you think. Please don't be sorry. She will understand soon enough and I know she can't remain angry with me for too long." I said.

"If you want to be with her, you are free to go. I will be okay alone."

"No Shipra, I won't leave you. I will be always with you." I assured her.

The next morning, Shipra's father reached the hospital. When he saw Shipra, he fainted. We managed somehow to revive him. The protests at the Ramlila Maidan turned into a big movement. Students from various schools and colleges gathered the whole country seemed to be in support of Shipra. Pratap and Sandeep were arrested the next day and were put behind bars. Shipra's father was happy to know that I had agreed to marry Shipra. My father supported my decision too. My mother was not in agreement at first, but soon obliged. Naina took time but she understood me. We are now best friends.

Epilogue

❄ ❄ ❄

"There is nothing about Naghma or the Muzaffar Nagar riots in this book", said Yogesh sir, flapping the last few pages of the book.

"Yes, sir. What's Naghma's story?" Alok sir asked.

"How do I know? Naghma's story can only be told by this person." He indicated towards the bed on which Chandan was lying unconscious.

"It's six in the morning, sir. The whole night passed away reading his story." Archana ma'am said.

At the same time a guard entered the room and after wishing everyone a good morning, said, "A boy and a girl are waiting at the gate. Their names are Kaushal and Anjali. They are saying that they know this man and that they identified his car parked outside."

"Bring them inside, immediately", said Yogesh sir.

Kaushal and Anjali entered in the room and touched everyone's feet.

When Anjali saw Chandan, her eyes grew moist, "I have never seen him so sombre. He always had a smile on his face before. Funny guy, used to make everyone around him laugh but now…." She left the sentence hanging for a bit, then added, "I am partly responsible for this piteous condition of his."

"You are not as much at fault as the love of that Muslim girl." Kaushal told her sadly.

"Are you talking about Naghma?" Saurav sir asked curiously.

"Yes sir." Kaushal nodded.

"What's the story of Naghma? Why was Chandan screaming her name in the middle of the night? How are either of them connected to the Muzaffar nagar riots?" Alok sir asked.

"I will tell you everything, sir. It's a long story. It starts with..." Kaushal shut his eyes to start narrating a most painful story of Naghma and Chandan.

What is the story of Naghma and Chandan? What happened to them during the Muzaffar Nagar riots? Who is Naghma? Where is she now? Why was Chandan shouting her name out loud? How is Anjali responsible for his piteous condition? Where does Kaushal fit into the story?

To know the answers to these questions, read GYAN SINGH's next novel.

NAGHMA
(A LOVE STORY OF A MUSLIM GIRL AND A HINDU BOY)